Consider it like a fresh new canvas. The more creative you are, the better your chances of finding him!

It happened at the same time. I was stabbing the tongue as the cage fell. I managed to get loose just in time to catch hold of the platform. The enslaved beast plunged out of sight, squealing in horror.

I pulled myself up on the platform and closed my eyes. Blackness filled my mind as I began my imaginings. First the walls shook, then the structure began to break apart. I could hear a loud siren wailing its alarm as the rest of the cages began to drop, one by one. My platform was no longer stable, and I, too, began to fall.

As I fell, I could see Sil grab a hold of Celeste and race to the edge of the terrace. There were near chaotic reactions spreading through the sector. The fighting was still in progress, and from the looks of it, the prisoners were winning.

Look For Other **Mystic Deja** Titles
By Tina M. Randolph

#2 Mecca of Ice
#3 Future Within

Mystic Deja

Maze of Existence

Written and Illustrated By
Tina M. Randolph

Rhapsody Publishing

Rhapsody Publishing

Sugar Land, Texas 77498

MYSTIC DEJA: MAZE OF EXISTENCE

Text and illustrations Copyright © 2002 by Tina M. Randolph
All rights reserved. MYSTIC DEJA and associated logos are trademarks and/or registered trademarks of Rhapsody Publishing.

AGES 10 AND UP

www.rhapsodypublishing.com
www.tinamrandolph.com

No part of this book may be reproduced, stored in a retrieval system, or transmitted by any means, electronic, mechanical, photocopying, recording, or otherwise, without written permission from author. For information address Rhapsody Publishing.

ISBN-13: 978-1-59109-416-6
ISBN-10: 1-59109-416-X

Visit us on the web! www.mysticdeja.com

Cover Design and Inside Cover by
Tina M. Randolph
Photography by Bernadette Dare

Printed in the U.S.A.

First Printing, October 2002

Second Printing, October 2016

"Inside the maze there are no limits, no boundaries, where you could go anywhere your creative thoughts could take you."
-Tina M. Randolph

For my parents Willie and Jimmie Mae Butler
who were my constant inspiration.
And thanks be to God for the Creation of Life

CONTENTS

One
The Oldest Man ◆ 1

Two
Secret Sole Receptacle ◆ 14

Three
Professor Onyx Returns ◆ 21

Four
The Underwater Room ◆ 31

Five
The Sleepy Koala ◆ 40

Six
Inside the Maze ◆ 47

Seven
The Edge of Eyeon ♦ 57

Eight
Becoming an Artisan ♦ 63

Nine
The Door Keeper ♦ 75

Ten
Hairy Troluk Man-Eaters ♦ 82

Eleven
Unleash the Chaos ♦ 91

Twelve
Hucki Muck Swamplands ♦ 99

Thirteen
The Rescuer's Chariot ♦ 110

Fourteen
Mysterious Coral Reef ◆ 117

Fifthteen
Koala Corner ◆ 127

Sixteen
Mental Reign ◆ 138

Seventeen
Make Ready Your Mind ◆ 151

Maze of Existence

One
The Oldest Man

Lately my father, Dr. Octavius Chanel, has been showing signs of being a real mad scientist. He has been locked in his science laboratory for more than three weeks, coming out for his favorite snack of tuna fish and tortilla chips no more than twice daily. Yesterday evening, I saw him carrying in bulky containers of snakes, lizards, parrots, and other exotic animals—I guess to keep him company, since my mother and newborn brother died just days before New Year's Eve. The doctor said she didn't suffer much—screaming violently as she did—for 28 grueling hours.

Just like Octavius, I've been mentally jaded, constantly reaching back, remembering things the way they used to be, before that sinister character I call the *"Heart Tickler"* descended upon them from another dimension. That soaring metallic *"creature feature"* with his mechanical outstretched arms and rotating fingers, spinning wildly back and forth, is the keeper of souls, the Grim Reaper's companion, lurking idly in hospital rooms, hovering aimlessly over sick beds. He uses just the right tools at just the right time to tinker with patients until something breaks, and shuts down all together.

Lying awake at night, I've tried to keep from having these nightmares that seemed to be ridiculously real. One eerie late hour, a wee, biddy baby burst into my dreams. His plump little figure froze in mid air as he hung by a string from the Tickler's hollow hand. With a tiny palm, he reached out to me, as he was plucked by his diaper and tossed into a swinging satchel. He cried no human tears, filling me with a newfound sense of confidence and peace. *How composed he looked!*

The glimpse into my own existence has always been intense. Sometimes, through random encounters of prophetic *déjà vu*, I can sense my ancestors. I've witnessed African tribesmen hunting leopards in the hot jungles while their women washed clothes under waterfalls, singing the melodious songs of heroism; I've seen Irish aristocrats smoking heavily scented cigars by the dim light of a crystal chandelier while contemplating political strategies and laughing away their fears; I've watched Cherokee Indians huddled together

THE OLDEST MAN

by the warm, open fire, as the wintry sky beat down on their ten-foot teepees.

I have even felt the calm tranquility that my great, great grandmother Kanelia felt as she meditated at the summits of steep cliffs overlooking mountainous plains. Her age was seen in her long, gray tresses of hair, flowing like waves of silk. She held cosmic knowledge in those thoughtful, emerald eyes. I couldn't help noticing how deeply she smiled, as she opened her eyes to the soft blankets of white snow, drifting from the edge of valleys where buffalos roamed.

I've never met her or even seen her, for she died before I was born. But I know her, because part of her being, memories and all, are hidden somewhere deep within me.

As the morning sun chased away the past night's shadows, Joshua, my "Boo," and I were watching cartoons when he unexpectedly said, "You should see a therapist."

For a long moment I looked at him thoughtfully. "I guess you're *right*," I answered. The pressure of my dwindling family tree was now a burden that had me so mesmerized, I literally could not refuse.

Always meticulously neat, Joshua paid strict attention to detail. A tall, handsome guy of nineteen, he concentrated heavily on outdated and rare books, guitar music, and unique magician's stunts. "Miracles of a lesser god," he would say. Though Joshua thought highly of the great Harry Houdini, he preferred to perform street magic and some good, old-fashioned card tricks.

"I'm *glad* you agree," he said, "I'll go with you." He pulled out his short pick and touched the strings of his Les Paul lightly.

"But do we have to go *now*?" I interrupted. "I don't feel like doing anything today."

"That is precisely why I think you need help," was his reply. "You haven't felt like doing *anything* for days."

"Why should I?" I asked.

"Trust me, Déjà. You need to get back to your normal self. This new you just isn't any fun."

Sensing my hesitation, Joshua stated, "Oh come on, what's the *worst* that could happen?"

"Well, all right," I replied coolly, standing up to shake the stiffness out of my limbs. "Let's leave now. Might as well get some fresh air." Those keenly perceptive, troubled eyes seemed filled with a ray of hope, as he drove me to the mental health clinic.

For 20 minutes I sat staring distantly out the window, mentally recollecting fondly how my mom and dad used to stroll hand-in-hand through our splendorous garden, while I ran about busily gathering fresh flowers, enjoying the vibrancy of the sunlit sky. I could hear the pleasant sounds of chirping beetles making such a soothing song, that I soon drifted off to sleep.

My dream took a familiar shape, and brought my mind

THE OLDEST MAN

from the past to the present, finally resting again in the car's interior—Joshua's form and the whirling trees that passed blurrily by on opposite sides of the freeway. Joshua sat perfectly poised and not too relaxed, as he cautiously kept his mind on the long road that stretched forth as far as the eye could see.

"Joshua, what's *that?*" I exclaimed, trying desperately to get him to slow down, but not getting his attention at all. I noticed *he was* looking at the street.

"STOP!" I yelled, grabbing the dashboard and steadying myself for the imminent crash, but the car kept rolling forward, as if nothing *unusual* was hovering in the middle of the highway.

I saw him plain as day. He was *old.* He was perhaps the oldest man I had ever seen. Old like Methuselah, who lived for *nine hundred years.* His wrinkled skin was full of tiny sparkles of vibrant gleaming stars, as if he were wearing a whole jar of body glitter. He was almost completely covered by exceedingly long, blue-white, shaggy hair, which seemed to shine and twinkle.

For a brief moment, time seemed to slow down, just long enough for him to plunge his scrawny body's head through the windshield.

Then the most startling thing happened—*he reached right down and grabbed my hand!*

"This way," he exclaimed, and the next thing I knew, I was diving into a pool of murky water.

I found myself swimming fast toward the ocean's floor. Then, as I turned to miss bumping into a beady-eyed trilobite wiggling pass my right foot, I realized something extraordinary: *I was still breathing regularly.* As we approached the sandy bottom I noticed a thick bed of fat, lazy jellyfish.

"Follow me," the old man floated in front of me, pointing his finger toward the surface. He led me to a large rock, stationed in the middle of what seemed like nowhere. I pulled myself up on it and gazed out at the scene. Up above, the sky was a dark purple color, almost pitch black, but somewhere in-between the sky and the sea, a powerful, bright, amazing light descended, warming my dripping-wet skin.

The old man smiled at me. It felt like he could *see through me*, as if my thoughts were *funny*. "Call me Zim Logi," he grinned with a wide mouth showing no teeth. "I have something to show you." I noticed he was wearing a bulky, cerulean robe that seemed much longer than his little legs should be.

"Well, what is it?" I asked.

"*Wait* and you'll *see*. It will come quickly," he replied, still with a grin. Gazing at the sky, he beamed. "Look, here it comes. Remember what you see."

The mauve haze climbed down out of the sky, swirling past me, faster than I could blink my eyes. Each cloud that hurled by turned a different shade, until I began to make out images in them, vague pictures. It was such a captivating sight that I wasn't sure, but one of the images resembled *Octavius*. He was standing at the edge of a steep precipice, gazing into a voluminous hole layered beneath a thick, misty fog.

Gasping, I yelled, "NO DADDY, DON'T!" but it was too late. He didn't seem to hear me anyway, as he dived head first, plunging into the mysterious pit.

My mind was spinning. I wanted to let go of my fears and jump in after him. I was startled to see Zim Logi smiling triumphantly. Looking into his reassuring eyes, I gradually began to understand. "You *must* remember," he was saying.

Nodding my head, I said, "I won't forget."

A sense of weightlessness filled my body as I followed, experiencing a ghostly numbness that shook me from my sleep.

The next moment I sat up bewildered as Joshua pulled into the clinic's parking lot. "Girl, *you sleep hard*," he teased.

The clinic was located on the outskirts of Houston, Texas. It was a tranquil and private spot, where a person could rest from the stress of the city. Joshua and I walked down a long, white corridor to a small room with a sign that read Dr. Pauline Shanavy. Once we were seated on a cherry leather sofa, a tall, slim, dark-haired woman walked into the room and sat down in front of us.

Dr. Shanavy was dressed in an indigo pantsuit with a paisley silk scarf and diamond flower pendant that I'm sure cost a fortune. Her eyes seemed dull like a raggedy old doll.

"So tell me what's *troubling* you," she asked, staring inquisitively behind pricey, gold-plated glasses. I glanced at Joshua uneasily.

"*Go on*, tell her how you feel," Joshua interjected. He put his hand on mine for support.

Immediately my right leg started to quiver—a nervous habit. "Well, it started with my mother's death," I began, "First of all, my Daddy has been up all night doing these *strange* experiments. I can hear him making noise in his laboratory. And I have a bad feeling that something awful is about to happen."

"What makes you think this?" she asked. "Where is the *fear* coming from?"

"I'm not quite sure."

I gazed annoyed out the open window at the violet-green swallows whose chirps seemed to get louder as the time went by. "Probably because I keep having nightmares about my mother and baby brother's death. My dreams seem so real. I don't know whether I am asleep, awake, or somewhere in between. And my dad, I don't know what to do about him. Both of us are going through our own grief issues right now. It's like talking to a brick wall. I don't even try to communicate with him anymore."

Dr. Shanavy sat quietly for a moment, vigorously taking notes. Her serious, pale face showed no emotion. After she had finished writing, she took off her glasses. "What do you *mean*, you don't *know* whether you are *asleep* or *awake*?" she asked. "Can you explain?"

"Ok, well this is what's wrong," I scratched my now-aching head. As I turned to her I said, "My dreams are too real—almost three-dimensional. Most visions give me the feeling I'm experiencing somebody else's thoughts; like I'm living through them—similar to déjà vu. It can be pleasant at times, but lately, it hasn't been."

Joshua started to speak, paused briefly, then looked at me surprised, as if I had said I was seeing ghosts.

"How often does this occur?" the doctor went on, unmoved.

"Two or three times a week."

Dr. Shanavy sat in deep thought. She was already figuring how to put it to me gently that I would need constant supervision and lots of sedatives.

After what seemed like forever, she spoke. "You are experiencing what is called *post-traumatic stress syndrome*," she explained. "It's quite common among people who have been traumatized. It's expected with the great loss you've recently suffered. I'll write a prescription to help you sleep and I suggest you get plenty of rest. Call me if you think you might want to harm yourself, but other than that you'll be just fine. Oh, look, time's up."

She smiled and led us to the door, handing me a slip of white paper.

Joshua and I reached the car and headed for home. Although the day was still young, I had suddenly felt fatigued and wanted to sleep for the next 24 hours. All in all, my afternoon had been most disappointing. I felt as if I hadn't gotten anything accomplished. Dad was still going to stay locked up in his laboratory, and I was definitely considering being in my room for the rest of the year. This was surely becoming somewhat of a routine for the both of us.

After I got home, I made my way to my room, turned off the light, jumped on the canopy bed and dozed off.

That night, I awakened to the annoying sound of the telephone. Immediately, I sprang out of bed, spinning around, franticly trying to figure where I'd left the receiver. I didn't end up finding it until I sat back down a moment to think.

"Hello," I said groggily.

"*Déjà*, meet me downstairs in the lab. It's *important*," my father whispered, exasperation in his voice.

"Okay, Daddy, I'll be down in a second," I replied, glancing at the clock on the nightstand. I wondered what could possibly be so important at 4:00 am.

My father's science lab was downstairs in the west wing of our huge estate. The laboratory was built in the early 1800's by my great-grandfather, who was also a scientist. Its walls were made of mahogany wood, its rooms spacious and well-organized. There were several quarters including an open, round space developed into a wildlife habitat, which resembled a zoo exhibit. It had a telescope too, one that stood out in size and probably weighted over a ton.

The one unique aspect of the lab was the simulated space room. Its imitation of the stars, planets, and micro-galaxies, were quite realistic and made you feel as if you were seeing the whole universe all at once. In the center of it all stood a suede, back-massaging chair, more comfortable than a couch, just right for lying down and pretending to be somewhere you're most certainly not.

The hallway was chilly and eerily dark. I passed my mother's oil portrait and for a moment, I gazed upon her face, remembering how she reminded me so much of myself. I remained there for a while, in a dream-like state, until I heard a loud burst, like breaking glass.

I was again wholly alarmed when I heard a screeching noise and then a bump, and a thud, as if something had hit the wall. I ran as fast as I could to the stairs and jumped several steps at a time to get to the bottom, being careful not to trip and fall. The west wing was deserted and rightfully so, since Octavius had dismissed the staff the week before. Rounding the corner, I gradually perceived the lab door slightly ajar and a bizarre twinkling glow coming from within.

"*Daddy*," I called as I pushed open the heavy door. All of a sudden, a strong electric current knocked me on the floor. Beakers and tubes flew against the wall. I shielded my face from the glass exploding all around.

When the commotion finally stopped, I rose quickly to look around. I was watching gooey liquid drip from a broken vial when I realized something furry was moving under a brown cardboard box, scratching and pawing, trying to tip it over. I approached the box cautiously. It was beneath a long table so I had to bend down and crawl slightly under the table to get close enough to see what had me distracted.

I had hardly flipped it over when I heard another noise behind me. I recognized the sound immediately to be static electricity. Ignoring the pulsations, I placed my hand under the carton and pulled out a half-sized koala. The koala and I looked at each other. He blinked his beady, little eyes, puzzled. He seemed even more confused than I was. With his large nose, he sniffed the wasted chemicals, and his ears became frizzy and stuck straight out.

"How *did you* get in here?" I asked not expecting a reply. Despite his unexpected appearance, I wasn't surprised. He had probably gotten out of the recently constructed habitat. He was the latest and most expensive of the group.

I got up, koala in arm, and began searching for answers to what may have caused the disturbance.

Two
Secret Sole Receptacle

Holding tightly to the koala, I made my way through the observatory towards golden lights that constantly beamed. I found myself standing in front of a heavy, maple desk, sleekly divided in two, revealing a secret passageway beneath the floor. Curiosity led me to step between the counters. At this point I noticed a hidden stairwell and proceeded cautiously to its bottom. I wondered why Dad had never mentioned this before.

I forced myself towards an annoying buzz, and followed the ever-expanding passageway, pass many adjacent doors that extended down the hall.

"*Dad,*" I called, a bit bothered. In the dimness, I could make out a grand entrance. The koala gasped and buried his head in my chest. He didn't like the strange musty odor that permeated the air.

I looked beyond the entry to an area that was appallingly rusty and I was smothering to breathe. I coughed. The room was about thirty feet in height and fifty feet wide. The walls were made of hard metal and there were no furnishings except a few computer monitors, a table, a chair, and some kind of control panel. Standing in the darkness, I paused in wonderment. Then I noticed something looming in the shadows.

It was a massive, motorized contraption that held a glass sphere at its core. Inside the orb were a gooey gel and a thick blue liquid that moved around and made bubbles the size of golf balls. Mounted on top of the mechanism was a towering antenna, extending outward like the top of a flagpole.

I remained there, staring for who-knows-how-long, until I was aroused by the sparks of golden light. Without further ado, I went up to the machine.

The first thing I did was stick out my hand to touch the glass globe. At least I thought it was glass. To my kooky surprise, my hand went straight through. My fingers tingled. In fact, I started to feel little prickly hairs stand up on my skin. I felt a presence surrounding me. Horrified, I drew back and ran to find the light switch.

Mystic Deja: Maze Of Existence

"Wow!" I said after the room had filled with a glow.

In moments, I returned to where I had been standing. This time, I kept my arm inside its belly, waiting to see what would happen next.

Out from the slimy fluid flowed luminous particles that moved in the slowest of motion. It felt like a cloud of microfireflies, all floating in the same direction, swirling around us. A slight whisper made me turn about. It sounded like my father's voice.

"*Help me*," he demanded faintly.

"I want to come *home*," his voice continued to echo. "HOME." I looked across the room and saw no one. "Lost in illusions."

The sparks began to tap my limbs—like tiny explosions of water droplets. The koala seemed to be coming unnerved. Then suddenly I remembered something. My father always kept a journal. It had to be somewhere in the laboratory.

In a flurry of confidence, I went back the way I'd come, stopping briefly to leave my new pet in his eucalyptus-tree-filled environment. At once he began chewing on leaves.

Wasting no more time, I began searching through a pile of documents. I checked his desk twice and had completely given up hope when I spotted it nestled in the pocket of his lab coat, which was hanging neatly on a wrought iron rack.

Realizing my dad was nowhere in sight, I secretly took the record book and headed for a place of privacy. Once inside the koala playground, I hurriedly flipped through the pages trying to find a helpful topic. The koala had climbed to the top of a tree, curling up neatly in the neck of its trunk.

That's when I decided he'd best be called Coconut.

The diary dated back about 18 years. Upon examining the cover, I noted an impressive mystical emblem encrusted in burnished silver. Inside, the pages were still crisp and remarkably white; probably from some substance my father invented. Then I discovered a detailed drawing of the machinery I'd seen in the secret room.

The description read, "Sole Receptacle" (Gateway to the Mind's Eye).

I wondered what it meant.

The following paragraph went on to further explain the theory of the device:

> In the case of the development of creative power, the sole receptacle is a telepathic transmitter. After acquiring a blueprint of the subject's mental characteristics, the receptacle is able to broadcast back to the subject their own interpretations of existence, which lie beneath their subconscious mind, therefore allowing one to experience the essence of their imagination in real-time.

SECRET SOLE RECEPTACLE

Emerging energy from the mind's eye is called the EMERGY—the center from which creative power flows. *An (sole) individual CAN make a difference.

There was nothing else except at the very bottom, the words:

Consciousness cannot be maintained while in transmission mode.

Gradually—like a veil unfolding—it became clear.

"He has to be asleep," my head echoed. I felt cold bumps rise up on my skin. I grimaced, realizing the bizarre entry was leading me elsewhere in the house. I left Coconut sleeping deeply, and quickly departed toward the replicated space chamber.

Trying to put crazy notions out of my head, I proceeded inside, and without a word, rushed between two huge planets to find the massage chair wasn't occupied. The only place I could think of next was my father's master bedroom.

A few minutes later I was creeping down the mirrored hall that led to his suite. I went straight to his door, which was already open, and at once heard a shrill scream that almost scared me out of my bones. The screech was, as I soon found out, coming from a black cockatoo flying vigorously to and fro. And that's not all. I was soon to discover a large iguana clinging to a curtain by the window, and a short, pot-bellied horse that should have been included in the *Guinness Book of World Records*. In a flash, that midget horse was shoving himself under the bed, as soon as he saw me coming his way.

When I was standing a few feet from where Octavius was laying, I looked down upon his sleeping shape and realized I was probably too late.

Octavius was a brilliant man—above average in every way—even in fashion, he was inspiring. He dressed in Italian suits and always wore a fancy hat. His complexion was coffee brown, his hair wavy and black. Tonight his smile was roughly reversed under a finely trimmed mustache. His frowning forehead gave me the inkling that his dreams weren't unfolding as he had planned.

Suddenly a silent rage was crashing through my mind. I stood, miserable and weak, envisioning him soaring through a timeless void. I was recollecting what Zim Logi had shown me. I had no idea how long he had really been in this unconscious state. I reached out and touched his saintly face. In some way I knew that this wasn't right. He should have already awakened.

I clearly saw what had to be done—figure out how to use the sole receptacle. I had to save him somehow. Or would he come back on his own? Could I take the risk of losing yet another loved one? No, this time I would directly intervene.

Three
Professor Onyx Returns

By now the sun was rising, and I was exhausted. It was a long while before I made my next move. Finally, I called Joshua and my friend Kyra over for breakfast. I thought maybe they could help sort things out. A few minutes later, I stood in the driveway, waiting patiently for them to arrive. I searched my mind for the best way to approach the subject of the sole receptacle, without sounding too extreme.

But as I stood there, feeling emptiness, I realized there was no other way than to just let it come right out.

Kyra was a true friend in every sense of the word. She

was like the sister I had never had. Short, ruby red, jazzy hair gave her a stylish appearance, and went well with her witty behavior. When she showed up, she was wearing her favorite blue jeans and a hand painted tee-shirt. Her pale, cheery face immediately gave me a sudden boost of energy.

Rubbing her hands together rapidly, she smiled brightly and said, "I'm starved, so let's eat."

"Hold your horses. Joshua isn't here yet."

"That's okay, I can wait, seeing that you cooked anyway," she teased.

"It's too early in the morning for that," I said grinning, trying to keep an eye out.

"I'll bet you didn't even go to sleep last night," she returned. "You know how you are."

"Well, as a matter of fact, I didn't."

"What happened, nightmares again?"

"Something like that. I'll explain it over breakfast," I said. "Look. Here comes Joshua."

Joshua slowly rolled his Mustang convertible into the driveway a few feet from us, and turned off the engine.

"Hey you two, what's up?" he said, as he made his way over.

The wild wind brushed up against my face, stinging my nose until it turned a rosy hue. Behind us, the towering mansion blocked the sun. I could feel its shadowy hands keeping the cold locked in place, as we marched through the dimmest corner of the courtyard. Even the trees seemed bare, as if they, too, were defenseless against the chill of the morning air.

After making our way through a maze of trim bushes and lively foliage, we finally reached the huge front entrance. Entering the doorway, I felt warm again and instantly comforted by the presence of friends.

"You can both have a seat at the dinning table while I go get the food." I unbuttoned my long coat and pulled it off along with my black suede gloves. Disappearing into the kitchen, I emerged a moment later with a stack of blueberry pancakes, beef sausages and cheese omelets.

"Okay," I said, "here is what's up." I took a seat at the head of the table while bringing their attention to my father's journal.

"I think my father is in a deep trance," I said. I told them of the wake up call, the lab explosion and the discovery of the sole receptacle.

"You've got to be kidding me." Kyra shook her head.

"No, it's all here in the journal. See for yourself." I handed over the book.

"Wait a minute, that's impossible," Joshua exclaimed after reading the description my father had written.

"*Nothing* is impossible with Daddy," I assured them. "You can bet the sole receptacle actually works."

"Okay, maybe it does, but why can't you just wake him up?" Kyra asked.

"I don't know exactly. But I think it's because of the explosion. Something is wrong with the machine."

"So what are you going to do?" Joshua looked dismayed. He wasn't good at hiding his emotions.

BUZZ. BUZZ. Suddenly, the security bell rang out like an annoying bug chattering through the wide, old halls. I excused myself and hurried to check the monitors.

Outerwear back on, I made my way down the driveway to the grand iron gates, and found a tall man dressed in a long overcoat, business suit, and wool fedora hat. At his side stood a younger, stern-faced lady who reminded me of my high school teachers.

The courtly gentleman stepped forward and presented himself.

"My name is Professor Onyx Chanel and this is Miss Hawthorne, my assistant," he said, waiting to see my expression.

"Chanel?" I questioned, as I opened the gate. Oddly enough, the Professor looked familiar.

"Yes, and you must be Déjà," he asked politely as he reached to shake my hand.

Nodding, I glanced at him sideways and said, "Do I know you?"

"Only as an infant," he chuckled lightly. "I am your father's brother."

"Sorry, my father never called you by that name," I said apologetically. "Please follow me."

With a quick wave, Professor Onyx silently communicated with the driver of the long, antique limousine they had arrived in.

"My dad said you disappeared some 18 years ago," I said hastily, as we walked to the house. I thought about all the years my father wondered what had happened to him; how he grieved continually, not knowing whether he was still alive.

"Yes, I've been gone a long time," he replied. "I came back because I knew something was wrong." Ms. Hawthorne was silent. She seemed solemn, as if she had just recalled why she was present. She and the Professor exchanged glances.

We left the front foyer and the three of us walked into the great room. Professor Onyx continued, "I *know* what has happened, Déjà. If you don't mind, I'd like to see him *right* away."

"You know about the sole receptacle?" I inquired as he headed for the west wing, leaving Ms. Hawthorne and me to get better acquainted. I didn't have to tell him where Daddy was located, since he seemed to be showing an unerring sense of perception.

"To answer your question," Ms. Hawthorne replied, "*he knows more than you do.*" She sat down on the soft chenille sofa and stared at me with intensity.

I wondered if she was studying my attire. My choice of fashion was distinctively inspired by styles of the past, with just a touch of trendy vogue. I loved being fully clothed from top to bottom like the ladies of yester-year. At present I was wearing an all black suede jumpsuit, full-length maxi coat, top hat, boots, and gloves to match.

I began laughing softly to myself and said, "Will you excuse me for a moment? I have other guests to attend to."

A few minutes later I was sitting across from Joshua and Kyra, discussing what had just transpired.

"Well, if you think Professor Onyx's return is not odd enough, wait till you see what this diary can do," said Joshua as he opened the book to an empty page.

We watched in weird fascination as these written words began to magically appear:

Entry #55

I fear the end is coming. I am being held somewhere in the Whirlpool galaxy. Marooned on a desert planet without food or water, I will not survive. Troops of Silver Assassins have taken my wife, Jenasee, from me, and my attempts to contact Déjà have all failed. The Sole Receptacle must not be functioning properly or I would have been back by now. I will not give up without a fight. My darling Déjà, if you are reading this, I need your help.

"My father is trying to communicate." I said. "We should show this to my uncle and see what he has to say."

"Good idea," Kyra stated.

I had forgotten I'd left Ms. Hawthorne all alone to entertain herself. Strangely, however, when we got to the great room, she was nowhere to be found. We decided to find the Professor since they were most likely together.

"I wonder if my uncle can fix the sole receptacle," I said. "Maybe that's the reason he came."

"Yeah, but how did he know it was broken in the first place," was Kyra's response.

Joshua shook his head. "There's more to this than meets the eye. No way could the Professor have known about the broken machine if he has been missing for 18 years."

I had to agree with Joshua that his reappearance was peculiar and that he seemed to know exactly what was going on. Or perhaps he was using some form of ESP.

"Well, maybe my dad tried to contact him," I added.

I started to say something else, but was interrupted by the Professor who was coming from my father's room. Standing in the hall, studiously poised, with his hands folded behind his back, he said candidly, "Yes he did."

There was silence now as we thought about what he had just said.

"Meet me in the library in half an hour and I'll explain everything," the Professor continued. Nodding at me, he said, "Just you." Then he turned in the direction of the laboratory and walked away.

"Hey listen, I've got to head on home. I promised my mother I'd watch my sister this evening," Kyra stated. "I'll check back with you as soon as I can."

"Okay," I replied.

As Kyra left, I turned towards Joshua. His expression had grown distant, reflective.

"I'll be right *back*, I need to see something." I said.

"Okay," he murmured, as he pulled out a pack of playing cards and began shuffling them. "I'll be outside at the gazebo."

With journal in hand, I headed up to my art studio. I wanted to examine it further, especially to see if any new pages had appeared. I thought maybe it would help me figure out what was going on inside my father's head.

My art studio was in one of the highest towers that bordered our residence. It was a round room built with many large heavily tinted windows. The walls were covered with a mural painting and hung with imaginative art that I had created. At one end of the room stood a vast unicorn sculpture, and just to the right was my computer workstation. Next to the desk was a drawing table where I spent most of the time doodling thumbnails. A canopy bed, a book shelf with crystal figurines and a large easel faced the opposite wall.

I also kept a diary to write down my dreams. Habitually, I'd jot them down as soon as I awoke, so as not to forget.

I sat down on my pristine bed and looked at the journal

that I held in my hand. Could Octavius be waiting for me to respond? Surely, I guessed, he would know I was doing the best I could do. And like him, I, too, would not give up without great effort.

Turning to a sheet I had not seen before, I began reading:

Entry #56

The silver assassins have been hot on my trail for days, but I found the doorway to Aruna, realm of ice. I'm sure if I can make it there I will be safe for the time being, although, I haven't a chance unless I keep moving.

Entry #57

The temperature in this realm is very irregular. Last night the snowflakes swirled upward from the ground instead of down from the sky. And when I reached the moat at the edge of the city, I wasn't sure how to proceed, because what lay before me was an implausible sight. A wall of slippery spume flurried steadily at the base of the floating habitat.

When I leaped forward, I felt as if I was swimming

> in an ocean of mist. I could see oversized spinner-flies moving about in the waves of foam that surrounded me. There was no way of telling which way I was going. This mist was so thick I was able to push upward till I nearly reached the city where the Yabosaur live, high above the ground. Hopefully, with skill, I will catch a great Mockamoo, which will take me the rest of the way to the Mecca of ice.

As I skimmed through the pages, I realized what he was up against. I feared he would definitely go insane in his worlds of illusions and daring escapades. If anyone could help him, it would have to be me.

Rising, I stretched, taking a deep breath. After I noticed the time, I remembered I was supposed to be meeting Professor Onyx in the library. I could hardly wait, wondering where he had been all these years.

Four
The Underwater Room

With anxious, agile steps, I proceeded to the sliding whizport doorway located in the hall right outside my studio. It was another of my father's inventions, and since the house was like a castle, it was the quickest way to get around. I pressed the keypad on the wall and waited patiently for the transporter to appear.

The whizport carrier was made of pastel silver and fashioned in the likeness of my favorite seahorse, an ocean-rider pinto. It held in its interior a passenger seat, and its body was steadied by two ski boards that glided smoothly along the dedicated route. After I was comfortably buckled in, I gazed ahead into the brightly lit tunnel that curved inside the house's walls.

"Prepare for departure," I commanded, as the door automatically sealed shut.

"Destination please?" the soothing voice response system asked.

"Library," I responded, excited about the jolting ride to come.

Instantly I felt a rush of brisk air as the whizport carrier slightly quivered. A vibrating hum drummed my ears as the voice response slowly counted down to zero. After the takeoff my stomach became woozy as the speed of the carrier steadily increased. Soon I was zooming forward into what looked like a black, whirling vortex.

The long, circular transport tunnel spiraled erratically as I raced forward to the destination chamber. I passed through countless barricades before taking a steep drop into a huge aquarium tank. Along this route the glassy tunnel allowed me to observe schools of fish swimming idly about. Several giant, tropical, farm-raised seahorses swam beside the pathway as I cruised toward the underwater room.

The library, which was designed in the shape of

an enormous genie bottle, was completely submerged underwater. Made of thick, bottle green glass with a metal-carved exterior, it seemed to have its own time zone.

The ride stopped abruptly, and I was safely dropped off behind a doorway disguised as a bookcase. Upon my entrance, I saw the Professor resting peacefully on a burgundy lounge chair, staring below at the fish under the flooring. The chair was positioned in the nucleus of the room directly next to a winding staircase.

"Enjoying the view?" I asked as I crept from behind him.

He looked up. "Yes, can't help but enjoy it," he responded.

When I drew within two feet of his chair I paused and waited for him to start speaking.

"Before I left, ages ago, Octavius and I were working on a secret experiment," he began, "called the *Gateway to the Mind's Eye*. We were hoping to allow people the chance to live out their fantasies or imaginings by submersing them into a deep rhythmic delusion. But something went haywire. I discovered the link between mind and matter was unlocked, and soon I was able to use more than 10 percent of my brain."

"*Fascinating*," I said.

"In other words, the sole receptacle was meant for submersion into the imagination of the mind. Instead I became changed from what I learned from inside of it," he said.

"So that's how you knew what had happened to Daddy?" I blurted out. "From breaching the boundaries that held back your abilities."

"*Right.* However, Octavius never knew what I'd learned. Each individual's experiences grow from what they desire. So I decided, for me it was too risky. To keep from temptation, I chose to leave."

He stopped talking in order to concentrate all his energy on a book, on one of the shelves. Focusing heavily on the object, he reached out with his hand and the book flew right into it.

"I don't blame you for being afraid to continue," I stated in bafflement.

"Ah, *The Emergy.* You should study this book. The great science-fiction author, Ramón Bedeea, wrote it centuries ago. Your father must have read it a thousand times. It was his favorite when he was a kid," he said, handing it to me.

My eyes swept over the intriguing cover. It had the same distinctive insignia I recalled from my father's journal. I realized that, yes, I was now getting somewhere. My father must have wanted to explore, hence his reason for inventing the sole receptacle in the first place—to live out his fantasies from his beloved volume.

Having made up my mind, I decided to ask, "Where did you go? What have you been doing all these years?"

"I've been teaching overseas at the world-renowned Institute of Parapsychology, testing the brain, conducting experiments of my own."

Since Professor Onyx had not mentioned the journal, I figured he knew nothing about it. Dutifully I handed it to him, after turning the page to the last written entry.

"My father kept a journal," I explained. "I stumbled across it last night when I found the receptacle. I believe he wants me to help him. He tried to contact me, but I think the machine you two created is broken. Can it be fixed?"

"I've already had a chance to look it over," he said. "The problem is repairable. However, this probably won't awaken him from his sleep. You will have to go in and bring him to consciousness, while I maintain the machine. This means reprogramming for double mind reception, because the sole receptacle was created for one brainwave at a time."

"Will it be *dangerous*?"

"Not if you know what to expect. It will seem real, but it isn't. Use the book to help you understand your father's fantasy. And remember, you will also have partial control over the dream."

The Professor rose from his chair and walked over to the spiraling staircase leaving me to ponder his words.

As he made his way up the flight of steps, he said, "I'll be in the lab making the repairs. I promise to tell you the moment it's operational."

Before he left, I asked, jokingly, "Why don't you take the shortcut?"

"The whizport? No thanks. I'll walk. I'm getting too old for that sort of thing." He laughed softly, I'm sure imagining me riding the whizport like a roller coaster in an amusement park.

"Just make sure you give it a try."

"I will," he promised as he disappeared through the hatched entry.

Before opening the heavy hardback book, I looked up. The dome of the library was therapeutically stunning. I could see pass the reflections on the hard glass. It was encased in intricately carved metallic openings, like windows. The echoing sound of soft waves brushed against the sides and gave me a calmness, releasing some of my tension.

Returning my attention to what lay before me, I flipped through the pages of the book till I found an interesting paragraph in which I started to read:

> *The silver, android assassins formed a massive army that could not be destroyed. There was no point in trying to deceive them for they could read minds and perform great acts of illusions that were inescapable. Great Reign, their creator, was now leading the battle against the remaining Emergists. Zim Logi was one of them. To protect the emergies from being stolen, Logi used all of his emerging energy to form a protective shield around the city of Setis Mines, but the timing was off. Almost everyone had been turned into mindless slaves. The ancient Emergists and neophyte Artisans somehow still prevailed against the Great Reign that day, stopping him from becoming more powerful than could ever be imagined.*

"My father really was into this book," I said out loud as I

shook my head.

Folding back the tip of the page, I hastened outdoors to find Joshua, remembering I had promised to meet him at the backyard gazebo.

Outside, the air was sunny and crisp. The garden was a lovely place, as serene as it was beautiful. Petunias and camillas were encircled by white calla lilies that resembled wedding bells and hung low to the ground. From the top of the stone steps one could see a great labyrinth made of elegant trees stretching over the endless horizon. There was also a lake where a small flock of swans basked in the rays of light beams that swung down from the sky.

Joshua sat on the timber flooring of the gazebo facing the water's edge. I knelt beside him and peered down at the iridescent reflection of our diluted images.

"Come on, lets go into the labyrinth," he suggested. I could see he wanted to go for a jog. Beaming, I rose up and the two of us rushed into the maze's towering walls. We ran a little bit, stopping a few moments to catch our breaths. Then I lost him.

"JOSHUA! Where are *you*?" I called. "You *can't* hide from me."

There was no response. A shiver swept through my body as I stopped to look around. I thought I saw a shadowy figure up ahead. Then it suddenly vanished into the shade. I turned and went into the dimness following the trail of where the form had just been.

A thick, wet mist arose as a storm cloud moved across the sky. Enclosed at a dead end, I stood quietly listening to the rustle of leaves while the tickling wind brushed up against the back of my neck.

"Joshua!" I hollered, this time in a crackling tone. In the center of the lair was a garden bench which invited me over, with its reassuring stance. Intensely anxious, I started for it, and hurriedly sat down before I changed my mind. Staring blankly into space, I envisioned my father. How disturbed he must be. I wondered if he had made it to the Mecca of ice, if the yabosaurs were a decent clan and how well they were treating him.

"What's on your mind?" I heard Joshua say.

Startled, I turned toward him and glared. "Where did you come from?" I said roughly. "I didn't see you come up. *Didn't you hear me calling you?*"

He leaned over and kissed me on the cheek. "I never left your side," he said cheerfully. "You just didn't see me."

"Can I tell you something?" I said, brushing a curl of hair from my face.

"It depends on what it is." He knew I was about to go off.

"I don't like this."

"Uh, oh. What did your uncle say at the meeting?"

"Nothing. He just explained why he and Daddy built the receptacle," I said, deciding to keep the details to myself.

"Well, can he fix the machine?"

"Yes, but the Professor doesn't know how long it will take to repair. And anyway, Daddy still might not wake up. That means I will have to tune into the receptacle and bring him back to awareness."

"Don't worry, you're a dreamer. You can handle it."

"You think?"

Instantly the temperature dropped. The frost hit the air when I breathed out. I started to see snowflakes drifting down from the sky. I glanced around. Unconsciously I bit my fingernail. I forced myself to acknowledge what I was seeing. Horace, my grandfather, was laughing on the bench where Joshua had been. He seemed to be engrossed in a young woman wearing a long cocktail dress. She walked up beside him and whispered something in his ear. Flirting, I suppose. I heard the chattering voices of a dinner party. The charmed sound of violin music began to play giving me a warm, fuzzy feeling.

Another mystical déjà vu.

"Did you hear me?" Joshua was shaking my shoulder.

"What?" I asked annoyed, waking to reality.

"I said, will you be okay?"

"I hope so," I declared, with a sudden urge to pray. Maybe the Creator God will give me the strength to make it through the day."

Five
The Sleepy Koala

For the next few days, I kept on alert. But the Professor never called for my assistance. I was beginning to believe he wasn't making progress, and the tediousness of waiting was a task all its own. Though he worked on it constantly, the system still needed reprogramming. And eventually he found even more things to restore.

Two weeks passed, and I was on the verge of insanity. Miss Hawthorne had seen to all the Professor's requirements. She had sent to the school for the necessary equipment and tools. Other oddities were designed which had been arriving in the wee hours of the night.

Octavius had been moved to a stasis chamber which was placed near the receptacle for constant supervision. While he slept, I read over *The Emergy*, trying to prepare for the journey to come.

One late night, I was standing under a spotted gum tree in the koala habitat.

Coconut sat nibbling on a plant leaf in the branches above. Since koalas are nocturnal, sleepers by day, I knew this was the only time I could catch him awake. Normally he slept for nearly 21 hours.

I was tired of being lonely and decided to let him keep me company. The koala, however, had another idea. He had scampered down the tree trunk and was screaming wildly in my ear. Just because he slept quite often didn't mean he was quiet and boring. In fact, he was the opposite of dull. Now he was making scratch marks on the bark of the trunk.

I stepped backwards to give him some room. After a while he grew weary of clawing and began grinding tough leaves until he had eaten almost half a pound. Then he shambled back up the trunk, made himself comfortable, and though he seemed drowsy, he watched me apprehensively as I sat down to read.

Entry #58

The dwarf, longhaired creatures called yabosuars, have agreed to take me as far as the Timoe Dali. They claim the voyage will be long and treacherous. We will have to cross the frozen lake of Tippitoin and go underground into the caverns where the shape-shifters live. That is where I will find the next doorway. I hope the doorkeeper will let me through. The next dominion, so I'm told, is a lot more capricious.

I expect the Great Reign will keep trying to attack. My emergy is worth more since I'm an inventor. Never fear. Despite the ice storm, we will leave tomorrow.

This time I have replenished my rations and have plenty to last for quite a distance. I must keep moving. I am sure the silver assassins will find me if I stay here any longer. Déjà, please hurry. I miss you terribly.

Coconut looked over my shoulder. He clung to the tree with his sharp nails trying to see what I was reading. I hadn't even noticed till I felt his fur prickling the side of my cheek.

I grabbed him up and sat him in my lap so he could be comfortable again.

"Want to see, do you? Well, here you go. But you have to be still. Hey, don't make that face." I laughed as he gave me the cutest expression.

He was a good pet, and I stayed there with him until I could wait no more for my uncle's invite.

I decided to visit the Professor, and went there several times the next day, but he was working so hard, he barely noticed my entry. And when I did happen to catch his attention, he continuously fussed, "Stay out of the way and *don't touch anything!*"

"How is it going?" I interrupted, ignoring his demand.

"Everything is almost complete. The timer is still broken, as well as the identity module. But my main concern is the double reception. After I'm finished, you and your father will be transmitting different signals, which is dangerous. You could be going one direction, and end up in another."

I tried to ignore the growing feeling that I was in way over my head. What if I didn't know what I was doing? Would my dad be stuck like this till the end of his days?

After a moment the Professor said, "Octavius has lost all sense of the true world. He can't find his way on his own anymore. According to Pierre's *Theory of Synchronicity*, his mind's mental gateway is no longer a revolving door. All you have to do is remind him of the real, submerge him into it and he should respond."

"Is there anything I can do to help?" I asked, as I watched him slide an airtight cylinder, filled with a slimy blue liquid, into the heart of the receptacle's connective mainframe computer.

"*Read.* It always helps to exercise your creative muscles. Which, in this case, is the source of your power."

It's a scary thought, actually. Traveling anywhere you're inspired to venture—limitless, imaginative realms of existence. In a small way, however, I was kind of excited. I wondered what I would learn from my collective experiences.

After a fortnight, I found myself in the library, scanning as much information as I could into my hand held KRAMM com. That way I could check on anything, effortlessly, in case I got stuck somewhere.

Kyra dropped by with two books of her own. She went over a few facts about the Whirlpool galaxy and its neighboring planets, which I also scanned into the KRAMM computer. Since her father was an astronaut, she knew things about the solar system that the average person didn't know.

"You sure you know what you're doing?" she asked seriously. "I don't want you waking up a psycho."

"I know about as much as you do, but what does it matter," I replied. "I'm doing it anyway."

"I might come over, from time to time, to check up on you. Just to make sure."

"Okay, just don't get in my uncle's way. I'm telling you, he gets real grouchy sometimes," I said, pausing from my toil. Then picking up the book on science fiction places, I started to import the first of the chapters.

I didn't tell her or Joshua about my uncle's telekinetic powers. Nor did I reveal what I had seen him perform. The last thing I needed was for them to worry about what the machine might do to me. I mean, look what it was doing to Daddy. Obviously, there could be serious repercussions if something went wrong again.

Kyra smiled. "What's an Emergist?" She had caught sight of the Emergy book and was browsing through the pages.

"An Emergist is a master originator. They are skilled at sending out energy, making their thoughts a reality." I sighed, tired of the whole thing.

"Okay, so will you be meeting them when you start using the receptacle? That would be weird."

"You have no idea," I assured her.

"Uh-oh," Kyra grimaced, captivated by the volume.

"What?" I gave her a puzzled glance and waited for her reply.

"Says here you might be attacked by the Great Reign, and he will try to steal your emergy and then you would become his mindless slave. How funny!"

"Not so funny if it was you." I said. "Then it would be you going through these changes. And I could laugh."

Kyra leaned back in her chair and clamped her hands behind her neck. It was hard for her to understand what I was truly up against. She had no clue how the sole receptacle really worked, that in order to win at this game, I would nearly have to become an Emergist myself, that it would take true skill and creativity to defeat the Great Reign's assault. To really do that was a matter to ponder.

Six
Inside the Maze

Several long weeks had come and gone, and the house grew lonelier with each day that passed. The weather was turning frosty as the winter months slowly crept in. It was as if the environment were being charmed into blind submission. Uncle Onyx stayed hard at work, trying to reconstruct one of the greatest inventions ever. I spent most of my time in the library catching up on my reading.

Dad was still sleeping soundly in his unyielding abstraction. I visited him every morning before breakfast, then again after dinner, making sure he was not alone in the fantasy world where he had been marooned.

New entries were popping up in the journal now, and each one kept me on the edge of my seat. Octavius was still fighting the arctic in the ice kingdom of Aruna. He was searching for the next doorway that he claimed was a shortcut leading to Nydia, the secret world where the last of the Emergists lived.

My mother, Jenasee, stayed motionless in the recesses of his mind, a major part of his courageous journey, his will to be with her a constant, undying goal. Just like in a dream, he could never quite reach her, slipping away as she did, hiding between the moonlight and the face of the waters.

I awoke one morning in my art studio bed, to the sound of a message on my computer. I had slept there the past few nights, keeping busy painting pictures that I envisioned in my head. I sat up and looked at the LCD monitor.

Uncle Onyx faded onto the wall screen and spoke, "Déjà, there has been a breakthrough in the system," he said. "The program will now respond to both of your telepathic signals, so come right away so we can begin testing." Then the image of him washed out as quickly as it had appeared.

For a few moments I struggled to calm the queasy feeling in the pit of my stomach. I paused, realizing that the long-awaited journey was about to begin.

I was trembling when I left the room. I went straight to the whizport and commanded to be taken to the laboratory.

Once on foot, I climbed down the steps to the underground passage and made my way to the secret room. There was no sense in trying to calm myself. Once I was reminded of what I was doing, I would become nervous all over again.

Glancing around, I immediately saw Ms. Hawthorne. She wore a white lab coat as she punched in codes in the mainframe computer. She greeted me with a smile and nodded towards where the Professor was standing.

"Ah, Déjà, good morning. The time has finally come." Uncle Onyx whistled a short, lively tune as he set the timer in the computer program.

"Good morning," I said.

"Let me explain the process. You will only have 12 hours, until you get used to sending transmissions. You won't get sleepy right away, so don't expect any instant results. It might take 30 minutes or more before you see a difference in your vision. However, the gradual effect decreases with time. Once you have sent your impressions to the receptacle, your thoughts will be stored in this special organic compound that runs through it, called the *"Intrinsic Fluid"*. It is the synergy that makes the whole system work. After it is collected, it will then be televised directly to your subconscious mind. At this point, you will actually be submerged in another dimension, the one you and your father have created."

"Ok, I get the *picture*," I responded, smiling. Following his lead, I walked up to a high, narrow staircase that led to a lustrous spherical apparatus.

"I have designed a unique stasis pod; one that will indeed surpass your virtual expectations. Your experience—shall I say, delusion—shall be highly defined," he said, pointing to the mechanism above.

"The chamber has been strategically positioned directly above the sole receptacle's antenna, so as to channel the clearest reception."

I was thinking that science was a well-thought-out organism that made all the difference when it came to telecommunications. I was reminded of my part in the scheme of the plan—the role I would play to bring things to fruition.

"Once I do a brain scan, you'll be ready to go. Oh, and here, put this on," he gestured, as Ms. Hawthorne appeared carrying a silver ensemble. The suit was full bodied and made of a reflective material I had never seen before.

Puzzled I asked, "Why the suit?"

"Well, let me explain. With the help of Ms. Hawthorne, a top scientist of NASA, the chamber has been constructed with the latest in technology. Levitation will be achieved by the simulation of weightlessness. In other words, it is an antigravity suit. This is to increase the brain's response to the physical side of the reception."

While he was talking, Ms. Hawthorne helped me put it on. "Okay," I said, taking a deep breath, "anything else I need to know?"

I was sure there would be a long list of things to remember, but I was wrong. The goal was quite simple. Be creative. I would not truly understand these words, until I was really living the dream, facing a challenge head on. Until then, I would pretend to be knowledgeable about my endeavor.

"Just remember, it isn't *real; you are in control,* and everything will run smoothly. Consider it like a fresh, new canvas. The more creative you are, the better your chances of finding him. Oh, and watch your step, your signals may still get crossed and we don't want you slipping off some steep imaginary mountain," the Professor said.

With this thought in mind, I perked up and directed my attention to the brain scan contraption. Ms. Hawthorne assisted me as I gave it my imprint. A few moments later, all was complete. Nothing was left except to enter the chamber.

Suited up, I stepped anxiously up the stairs to the suspended orb that hung high above the ground. Steadying myself on the rail as I climbed, I reached the platform without a stumble and watched a circular hatch open up. Once inside, I felt even more anxious.

Looking around, I realized the walls were padded with cushions and there were no windows, nor any place to sit. When the door bolted shut, it became pitch black. I stood where I was, eager for something else to occur.

Suddenly, I began to panic. I wasn't much for being closed in. Now the time seemed to slow down completely.

Before a minute had passed, I heard the computerized sound of the countdown to one, but nothing happened. All was quiet and I was certain I would grow tired of waiting.

Then I thought maybe I wasn't focusing hard enough.

"Think," I told myself. There was no noise, no light. The canvas was empty. Sometime later, I wasn't sure how much, I felt light headed as my body began to lift slowly off the ground. I floated, drifting to the sound the brain waves played in my head.

It was at that exact moment I was beginning to see vibrant colors falling into a recognizable pattern. I saw a large pterodactyl soaring high in the clouds. It swooped down toward a tropical lagoon.

Beautiful and green, the water sparkled like crystals, surrounded by small, grass-covered hill formations, and a trickling waterfall. The extinct flying reptile flew into a hidden cave beneath the cascading aquamarine drops that fell from the steep summit. I could feel the cool water brushing up against the back of my legs. There was something familiar about this place.

Standing there, I realized my thoughts were directing the stage. All I had to do was visualize and instantly my suit transformed into my own rendition of an ancient Egyptian outfit. I always wore a long jacket and jumpsuit no mater what atmospheric conditions I was in. Nonetheless, it kept me comfortable and secure to have it on in case the weather changed suddenly, which, for *me*, it always did.

Staring down at my reflection in the water, I pulled a lotus flower from my hair and sniffed its invigorating fragrance. Then I proceeded cautiously toward the hidden crevice, leaving the magnetic indigo sky behind.

Inside the cave, I felt a cool breeze coming from its core. Following the narrow path, I came across a cluster of huge water lilies floating in a rivulet. The flowers twirled and swayed slightly with the rush as they drifted downstream invitingly. With enthusiasm, I watched as a polka-dotted, oversized frog leaped onto a lily pad.

I was knee-deep in water now, making my way over to the nearest flower. The water was warm to the touch, and soothing. Pushing back a vanilla petal, I stepped inside and lay down on the soft cushiony center.

A sweet fragrance filled the air and awakened my inner senses. I began to relax as my botanical craft shifted, drifting a little faster downstream, deep into the dark cave.

I lay there for awhile, watching the roof of the cavern pass by. I smiled as I recalled the enjoyment I had, floating in my canoe on the lake next to my house. Yes, I thought, this is a wonderful invention. But, I was supposed to be looking for Father. No time for recreation. I sat up in the craft and tried to find a way out.

While wondering about an exit, I came across a brilliant fluorescent glimmer of light. The closer I came to it, the brighter it became, until I could fully see where the radiance was coming from.

WOW! I thought. Large patches of glowing mushrooms grew along the walls. Sticking out my foot, I steadied the craft. Gradually, it came to a stop. I studied the area closely for signs of life forms, and soon discovered a few tiny glow worms. I crept further into the grove and the next moment, I found a small hidden crevice. In I went. I was surprised to see dozens of large glowing mushrooms everywhere I looked. A few feet ahead I saw a fat and sparkly one that I figured I could sit on for a while and think. I hesitated, wondering if it was comfortable enough. To my delight, it was just as I had hoped, soft and cushiony.

I sat down. The area was filled with various sized mushrooms and I considered for a moment if I should take one. Totally fascinated by their gleam, I bent over and picked a couple small ones and placed them in my jacket pocket. Then I leaned back on the toadstool, closed my eyes for a moment, and began to meditate on the beauty of the surroundings. I was pondering this when I heard a buzzing sound. Curiously, I opened my eyes to see a swarm of lightning bugs flying in the direction of another well-concealed entry. I hopped off the mushroom, and followed them with interest.

Desperately, I tried to squeeze through the new crevice, and found myself struggling for nothing, because it was too tiny to fit through. I did manage to see what was inside, although, after a while, I wished I hadn't.

I looked up at a gigantic lair made out of thick, muddy soil. There was something buried deep in the dirt. I knew this because of the round sack-like shapes that stuck out from the ground. There were hundreds of them lighting up the place. And the hideaway seemed to go on forever.

I heard a screeching, flailing sound, as if what ever was buried was trying to get out. The creature broke free. "UH, OH," I said, catching sight of it, *"I better get out of here!"*

For one brief moment, I almost fainted. I had a fear for much smaller critters than these. This one was about 3 feet in length. It had a fat stomach, big eyes, and sharp teeth. Believe it or not, it could fly like a bird, even though the wings on its back were miniature.

While it hovered in front of my face, I worked frantically

to get myself loose. Soon I heard more squealing and the flapping of wings. I had to hurry. Somehow, I had awakened the whole group. Suddenly, I pulled myself out.

Without another moment's thought, I ran towards the opening where my lily flower was waiting. I looked back and saw the creatures were not far behind me. They were moving fast and in unison.

As I turned back around I stumbled over a mushroom, almost collapsing, but instead landed on a larger one, and it broke my fall. Still the creatures were coming. I had to think. I didn't want them chasing me all the way through the cavern.

Gasping for breath, I leapt through the cranny, and found myself again near the edge of the rivulet. No time to plan. I had to move fast. Staring at the opening, I pictured it closed.

A vine burst forth. Then several of them began to grow upward. After I was sure it was concealed, I immediately turned and headed for the flower craft.

I was already moving downstream away from the nightmare when I heard the creatures screech out because they could not break through. Luckily, that was all it took for me to escape.

"That will teach you," I said. "Don't go sticking your nose where it might get chopped off." I laughed out loud at my stupid mistake.

I was well on my way again, back on a mission, and I settled down comfortably, knowing the adventure was just beginning. Listening to my heart pump, I began to hum as my rhythmic craft carried me swiftly to the edge.

Seven

The Edge of Eyeon

In the moments that followed the escape, I went over what I had learned so far: always be aware of your surroundings and be ready to defend yourself, because things aren't always what they seem. Hopefully, I had learned my lesson well.

The craft stopped abruptly right at the edge of a deep drop into what appeared to be an endless void. I was still inside the cavern's walls, probably at its core. There was no other route to take. I had reached a dead end. I stood there at the mouth, listening to the howling wind, wondering how far down the drop was, when the next thing I knew, I was falling.

I felt light, and an as-yet unseen force was pulling me further into obscurity: a black hole if you will. My body had become invisible to me and I could not see my hands as I groped in the darkness.

The unseen force led me to a cavity that, once I had entered, closed up behind me. Confusion ripped through my mind. I turned my attention to the rickety balcony where I was standing. It was attached to the side of what appeared to be a narrow chasm with steep cliff walls, encompassed by a gulf of steel-blue haze.

The wind blew fiercely, whipping my jacket to and fro. I stood uncertainly, examining the dim abyss, until suddenly, a winding stairway began to form from the dusty surface of the cliff's walls. I realized I could go up or down and it wouldn't make much of a difference, because I had not a clue as to where I was headed.

My situation didn't look good. I had to summon all the strength I could muster just to make a decision as to what to do next. It was like a which-way book, and the path up the stairs didn't look safe. I was afraid I might fall off and plunge downward forever, ultimately forgetting the whole reason I came.

With just a thought, I changed my attire to fit with the weather, giving myself a long, brown bomber jacket, flying cap, and original, WWI goggles which rested on top of my cap.

Shielding myself from the lash of the wind, I started going

up, hoping I would eventually reach the summit. I tried not to look down for fear I might become nauseous and loose my footing. If I did manage to slip and fall, who knew where I'd end up? I didn't want to find out. To make sure, I took careful, planned steps, occasionally knocking off a rock or two, which plummeted into the nothingness below.

Round and round I went. The spiraling stairway seemed to have no end. The scenery never changed, and I had seen all the terrain could offer. It was so narrow that it took only a short while to encircle.

To keep track of my travels, I envisioned a small timer on my jumpsuit belt and checked it the moment it was created. According to the clock, I had been submerged for 3 hours and 15 minutes. Unfortunately though, I had not come any closer to my goal and was beginning to feel a bit disheartened when suddenly, the highland appeared. Finally, I had reached the summit.

Stationed at the rim of the chasm, I listened to the weeping air currents whispering its name, Eyeon. I stood silently for awhile trying to distinguish anything I could in the surrounding firmament. I saw another terrain far away. But I could not see clearly enough through the mist, so I reached out with my mind and fashioned a pair of binoculars.

The instant they appeared I put them to my eyes and began to focus on an object up ahead. At first I thought it was a giant mountain, but then I saw it was floating on air.

It was like a piece of the earth had left its abode and

ascended out to nowhere. Attached to half of the mirrored terrain was a gigantic bubble that, at another moment's glance, seemed to vanish.

I walked to the center of the plateau and sat on the grimy ground. During the next few minutes I contemplated my situation. Dust particles moved over the earth, cruelly stinging my eyelids. Wiping my eyes I stared at the horizon. It came from an empty space and lit up the atmosphere with passion. I was hungry now, and my stomach told me I must find something to fill it. On my shoulders, I made a large backpack materialize, filled with much-needed supplies.

Digging through its contents, I pulled out the journal and a delicious green apple. I took a big bite, then opened the journal and began scanning its pages. I was sure I had seen a drawing of a one-man machine my father had invented for flying. He had quite a few nifty contraptions that just might come in handy out here.

"Perfect," I said tapping the page. "Just what I was looking for. A *Jet-wing Hover Bike*."

There it was, laid out in detail. I knew I would have no

problem making it. After examining the sketches in detail, I read its description:

Jetwing Hover Bike

A flying machine designed for long distances through the skies. Lightweight and easy to handle, this bike functions as would a small aircraft, with numerous safety features in case of emergency. I have also added a few luxury items, which include a digital sound and video system, and helmet monitor for viewing telecasts.

Getting myself in gear, I put the image in my mind. As soon as I had added the remaining touches, it came into being as if it had already been.

Switching on the headlights, I mounted the bike and began to study the dashboard. Everything seemed to be working. After a pause, I put on the helmet and turned on the monitor in search of any signal I could tune into. As a telecast started to explode onto the screen, I turned on the jets and felt the heat of the smoke as it built up around my ankles. Then off I went, toward the mysterious territory in the sky.

At an accelerated rate, I sped forward as currents of air beat heavily upon the glass windshield. Some weird music videos sent shockwaves through my spine, as jabs of color blazed across the display. It held my attention for most of the journey. I could not understand a word it was saying, but I enjoyed it just the same.

As I neared the domain, I could tell the bubble was actually a force field. I had no problem passing through, which made me wonder why it was there in the first place.

Just before landing, I cruised for awhile and found that there were no extraterrestrials or alien homesteads. Nothing but a huge mountain and canyon filled the scene. The air was hot and humid. And there was no greenery to behold.

Back on the ground, I stretched out my muscles which felt numb from the trip. Jumping off the bike, I gazed around in awe. Since I was quite thirsty, I produced a water canteen and wholeheartedly drank from it. I wondered where I was and suddenly, the heat became profoundly intense.

As I was trying to adjust my attire by removing my jacket in my mind, I was shocked to feel a hand touch my left shoulder.

Eight
Becoming An Artisan

I looked around, trying not to panic, and was thankful to find a familiar being. Zim Logi sighed heavily and stared for a moment. He seemed in deep thought. "Well, it's about time," he said. "I've been waiting for you. You see, we have much training to do."

My mind raced back, remembering the dream I'd had where Zim Logi had appeared and revealed that my father was in some kind of trouble. Surely the mind plays mysterious tricks, for Zim Logi was not even a figment of my own imagination, but an imagining of my father's.

Nonetheless, I was happy to see him and showed it by giving him a big hug. He patted my back. "Boy am I glad to see you, Zim Logi. I think I'm lost," I said.

"Follow me. Come on. *This way*," he said, "We must start soon." He moved so quickly, I could barely make out where he was at any given instant. He seemed like a blur and after a minute, he was nowhere to be found.

I wondered where he'd gone. Turning around several times, I probed the area. I was about to shout out when suddenly, he tapped my arm and the next moment we were standing at the foot of a huge mountain. Zim Logi produced a walking staff, tall and unfashionable. Following his lead, I created one of my own. However, I was a lover of art, and therefore, lavished it with silver and shaped it in the form of a narrow seahorse with glassy sea-green eyes.

I stayed nearby, but always slightly behind, for he was swift, disappearing every other split second that passed. So far, I had managed not to become a bother, although I was growing increasingly curious of where we were going. Eventually, I would probably crack up. But, I was determined to wait and ask questions later, when we had reached our destination, which I was sure was a less hazardous place to reside.

There was silence as I tried to keep up, and for two long hours we moved cautiously up the mountainside.

Stopping for a brief moment, I sighed. Something wasn't looking right. As we walked, I noticed my vision was becoming distorted. Then the ground seemed to be shifting, and I wasn't sure where I was stepping. A few minutes later I was dizzy. Two of those minutes had been spent wondering if I was moving forward, or standing still as the landscape around me moved backward.

I suppose I should have stopped to rest, since my eyes were misleading the way. But I didn't listen to myself. I kept going.

With a scream of terror I slipped off the side. The pain shot through my arm as I clung to the ledge. I realized then, after being suspended, sustained from falling, that we had traveled an impossible distance in a very short length of time. I watched my silver staff diminishing as it fell. I saw we were thousands of miles up the mountain, almost at its peak.

"LOGI!" I managed to yell, "HELP!"

Zim Logi was quick and before I knew it, he had pulled me safely back on the ground.

Bent over and breathing irregularly, I paused. I was shaken, and frightened of the height we had reached. Zim Logi pointed towards the open sky, "We shall go this way. Are you ready?"

Puzzled, I questioned, "*Which* way are we going again?"

"We're almost there. Just a little farther to go," he continued, "Make ready your mind, for it shall be an inconceivable journey."

I stood up straight and frowned. I didn't like where this was leading.

"I don't see *anything* out there. Why that way?" I asked.

He stood facing the ledge and motioned for me to follow. "Things are not always what they seem. You will see, when your mind is ready."

At first I stared in disbelief as Zim Logi created as he stepped, a heap of ground made of gravel. And after he was out a ways, the path he had already trod departed into separate particles, vanishing into dust.

Stopping short, he turned back and waved his hand, beckoning me forward. "First lesson, creation of atmosphere," he said.

He stood, floating who knows how many miles high in the air, on a little piece of gravel that seemed sturdy and concrete. He waited as I pondered his words.

Nervous as I was, I attempted to reach out with my mind and create some gravel, but as I took my first step, I felt my foot slipping through the spaces in-between the shaky gravel I had made.

"Organize your thoughts, and then make them a reality," he said. "You are now an Artisan, and your craft must be an extension of yourself."

It reminded me of my own Creator, and His saying, "Whatever your hand finds to do, do it with all your might." So, maybe I should squeeze my hands, and close my eyes, and make it picture perfect. It could be done. Why? Because Zim Logi was doing it. He had shown me the way. Besides, I had to, since he was just going to stand right there till I made it happen. He wasn't budging.

I solidified the gravel, taking my time. No rush. I remembered how much I enjoyed nature, and all its many perfections; how I liked to sit and listen to its wondrous sounds.

"This is the first thing you must master. Create your atmosphere, and then keep it balanced. It will affect how well you perform in any situation that presents itself. Everything must flow in unison. Perfection is the key. You must get as close as possible."

I searched my mind for the right visualization. I knew it had to start with what I put in my head. That is where all my accomplishments are formed.

"Okay, okay, here I come!" I said.

It was a long few steps. But I had patience. Slowly, I envisioned perfect pebbles and how well they fit together. After the new course appeared, I sustained the image and pushed it outward, creating an addition to the first, until I was a few inches from him.

He was grinning now, pleased with my performance.

"Stay focused. Don't let go of the images. Control," he said.

Finally, I felt comfortable enough to stand up straight, and walk with confidence. He couldn't have been a better coach.

Even though I had a fear of heights, I didn't let it get to me. Together we walked forward, creating our pathway as we went.

At this point, I began to question where we were going. I still didn't see anything up ahead. And the farther we got out, the more dangerous it became, what with the wind that seemed to want to sweep us off our feet.

I kept close to my teacher, where the air currents remained calm, and worked on my coordination. I began wondering if we would ever get there. Wherever "there" was. But I was smart enough to keep my mouth shut. At least for the time being.

"Here we are," Zim Logi stated, "Our final destination."

I was confused again. I still didn't see what he was referring to. This time I had to ask. "I don't understand. There is nothing here."

"Just because you can't see anything, doesn't mean it doesn't exist. Look beneath the surface, for sometimes things are not what they seem. Be watchful, and always ready, because anything unexpected could throw you off course. And remember you are already there. Everything you need is right here with you."

In truth, I was straining my eyes for nothing. I still didn't get the depiction.

"To *truly* see, you must be able to *accept* what is being revealed. Try again. This time close your eyes, breathe it all in and be perfectly still," he said.

There I was, standing miles high, away from the safety of ground, trying to figure out what was delusional reality. I figured I must be looking at something, but I just couldn't see it yet. I knew it must be his domain, a palace, and probably a wondrous one, if it had emerged from the mind of Zim Logi, the most skilled of the all the Emergists.

I did as instructed. Closing my eyes, I took a deep breath and tried to relax. I began to smell flowers, and a warm sunny feeling came over me. This led me to become more optimistic. I had opened my mind to the unknown. With that thought, I slowly lifted my eyelids.

A dazzling rainbow lit up the sky. I found myself in the midst of a flourishing garden filled with alien wildlife.

"Where did all this come from?" I asked, as I watched a furry, bright-eyed critter jump down from a tall tree and scurry into the bushes.

"Oh, it was here all along. But no one is allowed to view it until now. You see, this is my abode. My paradise. And it is peaceful here. My creation has been in perfect balance, undisturbed for centuries."

"The temperature is quite pleasant here," I complimented.

"I keep it well tended, so all the plants can grow plentifully," he said. "Some day you will be able to create places better than this, once you have become a true Emergist like me. But first things first. You are now a Artisan, and there are lessons you must learn."

"But why must I be an Artisan, and what will you profit from it?" I asked this because I was curious as to why he was helping me. He seemed to be determined that I should learn all his teachings.

"I am helping you, remember, to find your father. It is his wish that he be found, and he is the one who has brought me to life. This is all his imagination leading the way. You need me, or you will never find him. He has been submerged for too long, and the longer you wait, the more complicated things become. You will have to stop the Great Reign from becoming too strong. Or else your father will never wake up, and this illusion will keep going forever. And with the Great Reign in power, life will be an endless nightmare. So you see, you *are* important. You *will* make a difference in the outcome of things."

"So that's why the Great Reign is chasing him?" I said, finally realizing what was happening. "He wants to keep him from waking to reality. Then this illusion will be forgotten, and he will no longer be in existence. Makes perfect sense. My father is the key. I must stop him before he captures his Emergy and takes control of him."

As I stood there, watching the splendor of nature Zim Logi had fashioned, something awakened in my mind—a powerful sensation of radiant energy. I began to believe in my abilities. I even felt a sense of joy, that I had been given the gift to create wondrous and magical things. I wanted to. It felt like my dreams could become a reality—my imagination boundless, unstoppable, and unquenchable.

My eyes swept over this new world, seeking to discover creatures I had not seen before.

"Go on, walk around a bit and see the new life in its infancy," Zim Logi said. "In order to create beauty, you must first learn to appreciate it."

Becoming An Artisan

I began my explorations of the garden by first heading toward a puddle of floating, reflective liquid. I became engrossed in this fluid because it broke up into odd shapes and then coalesced, sailing overhead like bubbly raindrops, except they never fell down.

There were many unique plants growing from the ground, some so large they stood as tall as trees. But what really caught my attention was a large orange and yellow striped creature

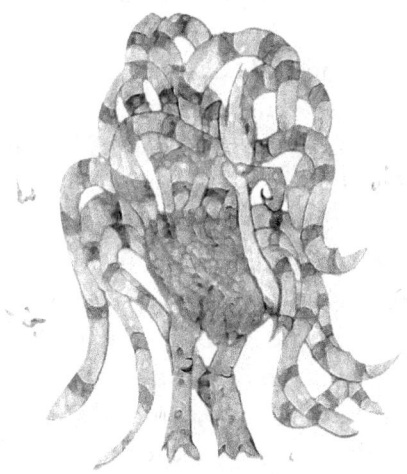

with 20 or more hairy tentacles that stretched outward like a peacock's tail. The birdie beast stood ten feet tall with many waving, slithering extensions. His eyes were black as night, but with a tiny glint of dancing light that showed it was probably as harmless as a dove.

I watched in awe as its many tails wiggled freely back and forth. Little puffs of green hairballs with eyes sprang up from the ground and flew by until they blocked my view. They were making a lovely sound, singing their song in perfect harmony.

I let one drift slowly into the palm of my hand, and watched it wink and fly away again.

"That big one's a Roxi and those fur balls are called Tikies," Zim Logi explained. "Tikies love to sing. And they never stay for long. They hide in the grass, so be careful not to step on one."

Surveying my footing, I followed Zim Logi to a large rock at the base of the towering rainbow.

"A perfect spot for you to practice," he said gesturing for me to sit and listen.

"Just a second," I said as I envisioned a thornless chair of rosebud weeds, and sat down upon it as soon as it was made.

Zim Logi stood upon the rock. He was quiet. "First you imagine. Then you create. Once it emerges, keep it balanced." He said all this as four elements appeared—earth, fire, air and water. He began to juggle the components until they swirled around and combined as one. Here, you try," he gestured, motioning for me to take his place.

I tried, but after the elements were swirling, the water fell on the fire and put it out. Then the air blew away the pieces of earth until there was nothing left.

"Do not worry. Emerging takes time. You'll get the hang of it. Practice here till you are the master of your imagination," he said assuredly.

Zim Logi was gone awhile, leaving me to my lessons. I repeatedly strained my mind, working my way up to sustaining the elements when, unexpectedly, I heard a beeping sound coming from my belt. Looking down, I immediately noticed the time. I had run out of it.

The elements disintegrated again as the scenery began to fade away into darkness.

Five, four, three, two, one. I heard the voice response system complete the countdown. Instantly, the hatch door popped open and light invaded the small chamber. I stared out the door, breathing hard, trying to shake myself back to reality. I was home again, and I was glad.

I turned and made my way out of the pod. I went down the narrow stairs, legs sore, and nearly fell down the last remaining steps. Uncle Onyx was there. He immediately reached over and helped me to a chair he had set out.

"How was your trip?" he asked cheerfully, "Did you make any progress?"

"*Not really*," I murmured, tired and aching all over. "But it was pretty exciting. The next time I go in, I'm *sure* I'll do better, since I know what to expect."

"Great, I'm glad it was to your liking. You will feel some soreness, but it will pass. You responded quite well to the new system I built. Get some rest, and we can start again in the morning," he said.

That night I lay awake in bed, contemplating my next encounter with the beings of the sole receptacle. I needed to find my father and fast. Why was it taking so long to locate him? This was worrying me. I wondered how soon it would be before I even got close to bringing him home.

I didn't stay awake for long. I was so tired that I began envisioning hordes of alien life forms and atmospheric elements, until I dozed off into my own dreamland.

Nine
The Door Keeper

The very next morning, I was up early. I made my rounds, stopping both at Coconut's habitat and my father's stasis pod. Watching him sleep made me even more determined to accomplish my mission. Without much hassle, I suited up and returned to my own stasis compartment, high above the receptacle.

Blinking my eyes, I could see the wooly beast floating horizontally to the desert sand dunes beneath him. He was stretched out like a flying carpet, wiggling his body back and forth in the wind. His lavender fur was long and wiry, with a thickness that matched that of an Alaskan husky. Beside him was a tall, wooden door that towered ten feet, shading my burning skin from the blistering heat of the sun. I was not frightened by the creature, but intrigued at its strangeness.

I desired to get a closer look, and walked up to him, until his eyes were even with mine. He seemed to be in a deep, quiet sleep, suspended in midair. He didn't even notice I was there, standing next to him.

The door had no knob. I leaned forward and tried to push it open, taking care not to make any noise that might wake the Door Keeper. Tiptoeing, I crept completely around to see what was on the other side, but somehow I ended up right back where I started, face to face with the hairy beast.

I stood there, staring at him, contemplating my next move, when suddenly, his right eyelid raised.

Startled, I stepped backwards, "If you want to pass, you *have to answer the question*," he whispered.

"What question?" I replied.

"The question you already know the answer to." This time the right eyelid closed and the left one slid open.

"How can I know the answer, if I don't even know the question?" I asked.

"You know the *answer*, because you know the *question*," he replied sarcastically.

"I don't have *time* for this. I can figure it out myself. GO BACK TO SLEEP!" I shrieked.

However, the problem was, I could not figure out what to

do. I was stuck. Transfixed on the door, I froze, as time seemed to stand still. Déjà vu again.

I saw him. He was standing next to the hairy beast just as I was a moment ago. I could hear his thoughts seeping into my head. "My father must have *been here* already," I thought aloud as I felt his presence.

Straining with intent, I listened to the convesation he was having with the creature.

"What is the answer to the question?" his voice echoed repeatedly, until it was a shrilling scream.

"You know the answer because you know the question," the strange sasquatch replied.

Octavius questioned him, "How do I get to the other side?"

Then it came to me all at once, "YOU ARE ALREADY THERE."

Slow motion. Crawling forward in time, like a spinning wheel of fortune, the encompassing dimensions around me curved inward and outward again, leaving me right where it had left me.

Glancing about, I was awed by the new world and its intriguing magnificence. The ground stretched upward sharply, creating ridged, mountainous boulders that leaped skyward, dangerously pointing their edges in various directions. The temperature was hot in some areas and cold in others. There was no wind, and no sound. As far as my eyes could see, the huge monuments towered for hundreds of miles all around.

I didn't feel comfortable at first, but after I had walked for a time, the atmosphere started to grow on me. My outfit changed continuously, maxi coat appearing and disappearing, fitting in with the climate as I moved around the large inflexible rocks. I did not know where I was going. Holding on tightly to a newly created staff, I noticed a change in the dimensional pattern of the landscape. There was a clearing up ahead and right in the center stood one lonely tree. The tree stood out above every boulder around it. Its leaves were remarkably colorful with various shades of red, purple, green, and blue. The silvery fruit that hung from its branches had an octagonal shape.

My taste buds tingled at the thought of tasting the odd outgrowth. Tearing a large one from its limbs, I sucked its flavorful juices with eagerness. It was tangy and spicy, like peppermint and chicken particles mixed with vanilla bean. After a few bites, I began to relax and sat down at the base of the trunk to rest. As I rested in that spot, I could feel the coolness of a slight breeze that constantly whirled by, making my visit there worth my while. Time stood completely still.

I began to meditate on my existence. I was becoming at one with the surroundings. I felt comfortable and peaceful.

I saw a temple palace, its huge doors opened up to me. As I entered, I noticed the tall pillars that reached almost to the stars. There was no roof. There were no other people there, only myself, and I took a seat on the cushiony throne pillow that sat atop a platform.

Looking out over a luminous garden, I breathed in the mystery of it all, while birds passed by chirping happily as they flew. My body had transformed back to childhood youth, and I seemed to have an extra eye in the middle of my forehead that lit up with golden light. I could hear the sound of trickling water drops as they poured out of the large fountain just a few feet from my throne. But I do not believe it was water at all; it was more like incandescent light particles swirling continuously, like a small storm cloud. There was something familiar about that flow of energy before me, but I couldn't quite put my finger on it.

My mind wandered, raced, and settled again. "The center from which creative power flows," I thought as I breathed heavily, listening to the rhythms of my own heartbeat. "It has to be my *Emergy—emerging energy from my mind's eye.*"

For a long time I sat in perfect silence, enjoying the moment of freedom. No problems, no enemies at the gates, just at oneness. I was invigorated.

I hoped to remember how to return again, if needed. After awhile, I had to tear myself away from deep thought, and move onward. Grabbing my knapsack, I began to walk back into the miserable scenery I had just escaped. The silence was unbearable. The stormy black sky seemed foreboding and dreary. I grew weary as I trudged forever onward.

Again, I stopped and rested, settling down under the shade of a large spiking rock. I searched my knapsack this time for the journal. There was a new entry.

Entry # 59

Déjà, I can feel your presence. You are near the underground city of Obilik. Be very careful of your path. Do not stay where you are for long. These people are very dangerous. Beware the hairy Troluk man-eaters.

If you can, look for the entrance to the next doorway. It is hidden beneath the surface. Meet me at my final destination, the center of my Mind's Eye. That is where we will find Jenasee. Then we can all be together again. See you there soon. Take care.

"MY FATHER SURELY HAS GONE MAD," I bellowed. It was too late. I was going mad, too. I could not hear my voice in this jaded dimension of a world I was in.

Suddenly, hefty stones started falling from the giant granite above me. The ground shook violently and I fell forward to the earth, trying not to let go of the journal as the terra firma opened up. Darkness swirled up like an angel of death, pulling me toward its heart, but I managed to hold on tight to the edge of the shifting terrain. Straining, I searched the deep hole below until I saw something menacing coming my way. Watching it draw closer made my hair stand on end.

It glided its motorized body toward me speedily. When it drew near, I saw someone inside its gaping mouth, working the controls. With a quick thrust, I too was trapped inside, staring blankly from the belly of this monstrous vessel.

"Where are you taking me?" I asked.

Ten
Hairy Troluk Man-Eaters

We spun down, further into the deep, dark abyss. The twitching, almost humorous, continued as the engine moved vigilantly to its earthy core. The alien man standing next to me did not utter a word as we passed miles of rock, grime, and undergrowth. I had a feeling I had just left the surface of a massive, synthetic square planet.

The dark preceded me. A protective dome shield hovered over a huge city made of limestone. Our vessel came to a jilting halt as we glided into section 8U2 and docked. A silver-haired young man grabbed my arm and helped me from the carrier onto the floor of the port, handing over my knapsack and journal, which somehow, mysteriously appeared inside as strangely as I had a moment before.

I was then greeted by a slender female dressed in elegant crimson attire, who led me down a brightly lit hall into a large, empty room.

"Where am I?" I questioned. The woman did not reply. Blushing, she excused herself and stepped out of the room, locking the door behind her. As quickly as she had gone, she returned with a tall, hourglass-shaped cup of foamy blue liquid. Not wanting to be rude, I quickly gulped down the drink, which smelled of icy fruit punch and left a delightful aftertaste.

Handing back the empty cup, I added a soft thank you and the woman again disappeared behind the doors of the great room, leaving me to wonder what kind of sinister plan was brewing in this quiet race. After an hour or two, yet another older female greeted me, also silver-haired, stern-faced, and attired in a shiny gray jumpsuit, obviously fit for interplanetary travel.

"I am captain Wanma Dane. We have a rule here," she stated. "All unauthorized travelers are considered hostile enemies and are not allowed on the premises."

"No problem," I said. "If you can just take me back to the surface, I'll be on my way again." I grabbed my backpack.

"I'm afraid that won't be happening. We have another law. Direct violation of our rules will result in immediate termination. Therefore, you must be disposed of at once. Guards, get her ready. The Troluks must not be kept waiting."

At the snap of her fingers, two big guards appeared and before I could get a word in, had grabbed my arms on both sides.

"You can't do this, I didn't know about the rule," I said angrily.

"Don't worry, you will die honorably," she laughed, turning to leave.

Immediately, I kicked the bulky guard on the right, furiously stomping on his foot, and an instant later, jabbed the other one in the stomach. "Arrgh," he grunted. I took off running, trying to find a place to hide.

I've got to get out of here, I thought, remembering my father's written words about how dangerous these people were. I heard the pitter-patter of their feet, just inches behind me.

I had forgotten I was not in an actual world. It did not seem to matter though, because my mind was telling me everything was real. In the hallway, I passed dozens of little girls and boys, and groups of teenagers all dressed in the same attire. Some of them seemed in awe and whispered amongst themselves.

"Did you see her? *Look!* I can't *believe* it. Someone should stop her," I heard them say. I didn't have time to wonder what they were talking about. I was on a mission.

"This way, and *hurry* before they capture you," a tall blue-eyed guy of about 18 bellowed.

Hairy Troluk Man-Eaters

I followed him without a moment's thought. What choice did I have? He led me to a wall that opened from the middle, then immediately slid shut. "Wait here," he instructed and disappeared back through the gray doors.

"I saw her go that way," I heard him say, steering the guards in another direction.

Thankfully, it worked. After the guards left, he returned with a smile.

"My name is Sil," he said. "I can tell you are not from around here. Neither am I. What's your name?"

"Déjà Chanel," I replied. "These people are out of their minds."

Sil laughed. "Where are you from anyway?" he asked.

"I'm from the US of A. You wouldn't know of it."

"I was kidnapped about a year ago. I've been trying to get home for some time now," he stated. "You know, they have a strict rule around here. Nobody can live past their eighteenth birthday and today is mine. You see, I've run out of time."

"What?" I replied, amazed at his words, "These people *really are loco*. You and I both have to get out of here then, because I've been 18 for some time now."

"Do you have a plan of escape?" I inquired.

"Kind of, but I may need some help. I will meet you here in an hour, and then we can discuss our strategy. In the meantime, stay clear of the hall cameras. I have to go."

After he disappeared, I decided to stay put. I didn't want to risk being caught in the halls. It didn't matter anyway, because all of a sudden, a red light, stationed near the ceiling, began blinking and blaring, alarming everybody to my whereabouts.

The door slid open and several huge guards rushed in with massive weaponry. I was taken to a large waiting room, and locked in with others, whom I guessed would suffer the same fate.

"We have four hours," a young girl about my age explained. She pointed to a digital timer on the wall located right above the entrance. "Hi, I am Celeste, and you are?"

"Déjà," I answered, aimlessly searching the crowded compartment.

"There is no way out. I've already tried," Celeste put in. I noticed the weary-eyed faces of all who were here. Huddled together, young men and women sought each other for comfort. Friends cried tears of sorrow, remembering the years they shared together, and some were quiet, waiting the final countdown to their inevitable demise. The room reeked of wretchedness.

Careful not to get too distraught, I sat down on the floor to think things through.

"Why?" unnerved, I blurted out, in a state of confusion.

"What do you mean?" Celeste asked.

"Why are they doing this? What could they possibly gain?"

"It's the *man-eaters*. The nasty *Troluks*," she said. "They keep them for protection."

"To protect them from what?" I asked.

"The Great Reign and his army of androids."

"I should have known," I admitted. "I've heard a lot about him. He is an Emergist."

"Not just any Emergist: the master of all. He has already destroyed many homelands, including my own."

"Were you also kidnapped?" I asked.

"Yes, but no one else survived. My family were all turned into slaves. I was found wandering around after the attack, by Captain Wanma Dane. She brought me here, and now, my time's run out."

"I don't understand," I said, trying to get the real reason I was being prepared for their feeding. "Why do they need the Troluks?"

"They are building an army of their own. An army of Troluks, to stop the Great Reign's attacks."

"But that doesn't make sense, killing us to stop him from killing."

Celeste shrugged her shoulders in agreement. Just then we heard a commotion of frightened teenagers as the door of our prison swung open.

It was Sil. One guard brought him inside, then quickly left.

"Sil, are you alright?" I made my way through the crowd towards him. He had a black eye.

"What happened?" I asked.

"They caught me snooping around the control room. I was trying to find a way to sabotage the system."

"Well?" Celeste looked hopefully into his eyes.

"No such luck," he responded. "They caught me before I could do any damage."

"By the way, this is Celeste," I said. "Celeste, meet Sil." They greeted each other briefly. Celeste seemed to blush as she gently shook his hand.

"Well, do you have another plan?" I asked Sil.

"Possibly, we might have a chance if we can get to the elevator."

"What elevator?" Celeste asked.

"In the feeding area, there is a 200 foot drop, and a secret door that leads to an elevator. I discovered it one night about a week ago when I was tailing a guard. If there was some way we could get to the shaft, we could climb up, or maybe use the elevator to get back to the surface. My father will be there waiting, so we've got to figure out a way to get to his spaceship," he explained.

I began to consider the possibilities. I wished Zim Logi was around to help me figure out what I should do. Looking down, I checked the timer. I had approximately 6 hours left. Uncle Onyx had given me 2 extra ones today. I wondered if there was any way I could stop this dream and wake up.

Well, one thing I was sure of, I should be able to do something to help. After all, Zim Logi wasn't training me for nothing.

"Listen," I said, pulling Sil and Celeste towards an empty corner. Do you know of the Emergist, Zim Logi?"

"Yes, Zim Logi is considered the greatest Emergist that ever lived. He is also the Great Reign's worst enemy from the old times. But no one has heard from or seen him for over 500 years," Celeste answered.

"Well, believe it or not, I'm his student Artisan. I don't know much, but I might be able to use what I've learned so far."

"You're right, I don't believe you," Celeste said.

"Give me your hand," I insisted. I was going to have to prove myself or she would mess everything up. Cautiously, she stuck it out, and I took it. Closing it firmly, I pushed it back, and said, "Open it."

She gave a look of surprise as a butterfly flew out and gently flapped its colorful wings. "You see, I do know a few things."

"Okay, now what?" Sil said. "How will creating insects help us?"

Huddling close to them, I began to discuss our strategy of escape. It would not be an easy one but, I was willing to take the risk. I certainly didn't want to have nightmares of being swallowed by a hairy Troluk for the rest of my life.

The red light came on again and a cluster of youths began moving about franticly. Two guards returned and started picking out a group of 20. Afterwards they were led out of the room, and the doors locked behind them.

"It's starting," Celeste warned, "we better get ready."

I noticed a guy bumping his head against the wall, and a brunette began to sob in the corner, tears drenching her clothes.

My vision began to look digital as the walls around me broke apart. I wondered if I should say goodbye. "No," I gasped, puzzled as to why I was leaving so soon. As my hearing faded, I saw Sil and Celeste talking to each other. They didn't seem to notice my disappearance, but I noticed theirs, the moment they were gone.

Eleven
Unleash The Chaos

Bursting from the vestibule, I yelled down at my uncle at the foot of the stairs.

"No, you have to send me back in," I said. Hurriedly, I bounded down the flight of steps towards him. "What is going on? I thought I had another 6 hours to go?" I questioned.

"You did, but I pulled you out on purpose. I've been monitoring you constantly, and I noticed a change in your stats. Something was wrong, so I shut it off early."

"You don't understand. I was making progress. I need to

get back to them before it's too late."

"Don't worry, I can get you set up in a few minutes. What's the rush? You find him already?" he asked.

"No, not yet, but I have learned a lot. There really isn't much time to explain, however. Maybe you can help me. Telekinesis. How does it work? Is it like using your emergy?"

"Yes, it holds to the same principle. But, instead of creating, you rearrange elements somebody else has already made. Basically, you need to focus on modification. Use your emergy to move, twist, bend, stretch and pull. You know, like molding a clump of clay into a new shape," he explained.

"I see, thanks. Now send me back in," I insisted, leaping up the stairs to my pod.

I couldn't believe how anxious I was. I wanted to return where I'd left off in order to help Sil and Celeste escape the Troluks. The imaginary world had become as real to me as the real world was.

"Okay, how about 16?" I heard him say. But I didn't respond.

Once back in, I started receiving images much faster. Sil and Celeste were still talking when I returned. They hadn't even noticed I had left them.

The clock on the wall neared its countdown. I knew I needed time to prepare for my feat, so I sat in a corner, and quietly arranged everything in my head.

Talking to myself, I repeated the words, "Imagine, create, balance and control," several times. Then I said, "You are already there."

When the alarm went off again, I was sure I was going next. The guards came in as before and began their second round of picks. Each person singled out was escorted into a straight line. I watched nervously as one of the guards, a tall mean-faced one, moved in my direction. He stopped short and paused a moment. Then he pointed at me and said, "*You!*"

Pushing those in front of him to the side, he made his way over and stared at me callously, saying, "You, *get in line!*" Turning, he nodded at Celeste and repeated his command.

As I walked toward the line, I paused, waiting for him to pick Sil out of the crowd. It was a part of the plan that all three of us be taken at the same time. When the guard passed over him, I started to panic. At once, Sil grabbed my arm in protest and pleaded, "No, *don't take her,*" and it worked. The guard took the bait and ordered Sil to come with us.

As far as I was concerned, everything now was going according to plan. Winking at Sil, I found my place in line behind Celeste, who looked distressed.

"Don't worry," I said, "It will work out. Just remember, I go first."

From there, we were moved from one empty room to another, each smaller than the last, until finally, we reached a corridor that led to an array of empty platforms. Behind us stood several colossal, rotating fans that made an irritating swooshing sound.

"Okay, stop right here," a guard suddenly barked. He

walked down the single file line touching the shoulders of every second person until he and I were face to face. "Step up to the X and the rest of you get back against the wall," he continued.

The lights flickered on and off. Sweat rolled down my face to my neck. Obediently, I stepped up to a marked X on the floor and turned to see the expression of Sil and Celeste, who had been instructed to stand against the wall.

They watched me with such anxiety, it made me nervous. Quickly I mouthed the words, "This will only take a second."

There were open thresholds in view. We each had our own separate one. As I stared through mine, I began to make out a figure hanging by a chained handcuff. I watched in horror as three long tongues came from the darkness and snapped the victim away like a fly-eating frog. I even thought I heard bones cracking in the distance, I guess, as the Troluk was chewing its prey.

There was a sudden outburst of murmuring as those standing in line with me were escorted up to the moving platforms and commanded individually to place their hands in the bloody cuffs. A guard was stationed at each post making sure this was carried out.

"No! Let go of me. Leave me alone," a blonde girl yelled, as a soldier forced her hands into the shackles.

My wrists had also been secured, and now my platform was moving forward, as were the others. Once it stopped, I looked around. It was hard to see what was out there. I knew there was a long drop below, from the whistling of the air currents circling the massive tunneling sector.

The light was dim. My hands were locked tightly in braces of steel. There was no way I could get unfastened, unless by some sort of miracle of wills. But I was ready for whatever was lurking, because in my mind, I had a perfect plan of escape.

The time had come to let go of my fears and begin the imagining. First I created a jagged dagger hidden beneath my maxi coat, tied by a belt strip on the side of my leg. Then I pushed out with my mind to bend the metal cuffs until they popped open, releasing my arms.

Just then a loud scream startled me. It came from the end of the line. I froze, stiff, as a large cage came into view from the other end of the sector. Its inhabitant appeared to be hairy and mutated, like a hunchback version of a disfigured frog. Its sharp teeth dripped a wet, clear, gooey liquid.

My expression turned to disgust as the stink filled my nostrils. His brown, straggly hair hung like tree moss. He opened his wide mouth, and grunted so loudly, it shook my platform.

By now there were screams of terror all the way down the line. Celeste was yelling, "Watch out Déjà," as a long wet tongue flew out in front of me. Quickly, I grabbed the blade and, with a measured force, I cut off the tip. The beast squealed in agony.

Turning towards the guards, mentally, I twisted the ends of the weapons they carried and yelled, "Now!" to Sil and Celeste who were awaiting my signal. For a moment, I watched Sil punch a guard in the chest. Then he kicked several of the others in a Kung Fu style. Celeste attacked too, kicking, punching, and doing some moves I had not seen before.

I felt another tongue wrap around my waist and neck, trying to squeeze the life from my flesh. I could feel the air leave my lungs. The Troluk flung me backwards towards its grotesque shape, ready to taste my skin in its mouth. It was like slow motion. The knife flew from my hands and fell towards the sector below. For a brief moment I was afraid I would have to suffer the mental pain of being eaten alive.

But I hadn't given up yet. I could hear the chains of its metal cage tearing from their hinges as I pushed with my emergy, breaking it from security and regaining the dagger.

It happened at the same time. I was stabbing the tongue as the cage fell. I managed to get loose just in time to catch hold of the platform. The enslaved beast plunged out of sight, squealing in horror.

I pulled myself up on the platform and closed my eyes. Blackness filled my mind as I began my imaginings. First the walls shook, then the structure began to break apart. I could hear a loud siren wailing its alarm as the rest of the cages began to drop, one by one. My platform was no longer stable, and I, too, began to fall.

As I fell, I could see Sil grab a hold of Celeste and race to the edge of the terrace. There were near chaotic reactions spreading through the sector. The fighting was still in progress, and from the looks of it, the prisoners were winning.

I emerged a silvery rope as if it were a spider's web. It attached to the walls giving Sil and Celeste a way of escape. As the two of them leaped from the ledge, I hurled myself rapidly to the segment below. I twirled as I fell. A moment before certain, psychological death, I slowed to a stop, floating directly above the flooring.

The walls shook violently. The remainder of the Troluk's cages dangled, swinging loosely from the chains that hung them from the ceiling. I could hear their howls as the creatures realized the possibility of an impending downfall.

Flipping to the ground, I was poised there, as part of the compound came crashing down, cages and all. The hits were tremendous, breaking open the pens, setting free the surviving man-eaters.

One enclosure tumbled a few feet in front of me, knocking open the bolted latch. Suddenly, I was again a target, as a hairy, Troluk man-eater charged toward me, fury raging in its eyes.

"This way, Déjà," Sil called out from the chaos behind me. Breathing hard, I quickly turned to flee. I ran, Troluk biting at my heels. I could envision its long, wiry, strands of hair, whipping wildly about as it flung itself forward, galloping towards its retreating feast.

I saw Sil and Celeste. They had made it to the elevator and were franticly calling for me to hurry as the airtight opening began to shut.

I sped, faster now, outrunning my predator. I barely made it as the doors sealed us in. Kneeling down, I tried to catch my breath. The Troluk pounded its weight against the elevator door. Sil had already pushed the right buttons and a moment later, we were speeding towards the synthetic surface of Obilik.

Twelve

Hucki Muck Swamplands

For a moment, we rose silently upward. Each of us staring through the glass elevator at remnants of the sector, as parts of it collapsed. Surely, the city of Obilik would still stand, but much damage was done. At least it would keep the armed forces' attention occupied, while we got away.

We were released from the ride at the base of a huge stone pyramid. As soon as we stepped out into the atmosphere, I remembered how much I detested its ambience. The chill of the air crept under my skin, while the hollowing sky yielded a blanket of gloominess.

As predicted, we saw a towering spacecraft in the distance. We rushed toward it, leaping over sharp stones, fighting fatigue, and doing our best to keep up with each other.

When we had almost reached the ship's entry, quakes broke out beneath us. The ground seemed to be giving way, cracking heavily in certain regions.

Celeste tumbled over, hitting the hard surface, and nearly losing her life, as a newly formed cavity grew ever wider. Without saying a word, Sil and I managed to grab her up and help her to her feet, forcing us all to keep moving forward.

I was certain that Wanma Dane and her fleet would appear, rising like a swarm of angry bees from their hive.

Nauseated and exhausted, we climbed aboard, buckling ourselves in the first seats we spotted. Through the view-port, we saw a hoard of starships rising from the depths of the planet.

Our get-away vessel was already in motion, lifting in record speed and zooming into space toward what appeared to be an electrifying whirlpool of energy.

"Hold on, we're going through a wormhole!" Sil yelled as the spacecraft started to shudder and shake.

Once we made it beyond, Sil unbuckled his seatbelt and motioned for Celeste and me to follow him into an adjoining compartment that turned out to be the spaceship's control room. "This is my father, Peg," Sil said, as he hugged his liberator's thick chest. He introduced us as well, mentioning how we had helped him escape.

Peg was a short, husky man with a dark mustache and a friendly look about his face. His eyes were deep and penetratingly familiar. It was as if he was a long lost friend.

"We'll be home in no time," he said, pointing to a planet on the main view port. "Your mother misses you terribly, son. She will be waiting with a feast of food when we arrive. I'm sure you guys must be tired and hungry."

As we drew ever closer to the planet's atmosphere I noticed a thick fog saturating the sky. The ship took a nose dive, going down into a brush of tall trees. It crept along its shadowy route.

"We are nearing the Hucki Muck swamplands," Sil exclaimed joyously. "I can't wait to see Mom."

To help navigate through the fog, Peg switched on a powerful headlight. Minutes later I heard strange thumping and scratching sounds from outside.

"What was that?" I asked, as Sil chuckled lightly.

"Oh, that was just a pack of flying whompas fish. They fly backwards and they are attracted to light," he explained. "Don't worry, they aren't that dangerous. And anyway, this is a sturdy ship. No need to panic."

I could hear the flying whompas flinging their bodies at the ship. It started from the back of the craft, and ended at the front. Then, without hesitation, they dived into the main viewport, sucking and scratching at the glass, trying to get in. They left large, wet, lip marks all over the area as they slid off, then dived out of sight.

"Is there water down there?" Celeste asked, after hearing a huge splash.

"Yes, this whole planet is made mostly of it. Nothing but swamps around here. There will be more whompas attacking the ship. Just wait a minute, you'll see."

Just as he said it, over a dozen more began to appear, keeping close to the proximity of the front headlights.

"Tomorrow, we will catch them. The two of you will love it. They taste delicious. Mother has probably cooked some for dinner."

Celeste and I looked at each other and made yucky noises. From what we could tell, flying whompas didn't look all that appetizing. Nonetheless, I was happy we had made it out of Obilik alive, and Sil was returning to his beloved homeland.

So far, I hadn't made much progress in finding my father, though. But I knew my journey was just beginning.

As we approached a group of dwellings high atop a colossal, moss-draped cypress tree, my eyes got big. I was immediately taken aback at the sight of it. It was the grandest tree I had ever seen, probably over a millennium in years.

Much to my surprise, there was a wooden platform. We landed there, and quickly exited through the side of the ship.

It was nightfall now, and stars twinkled in the sky. There were three large moons in the distance called space. From where I was standing, it was much needed light.

A short, plump-armed woman stood just a few feet away, watching as our entourage appeared. She wore a long, baggy dress, and a white apron that she reached down and wiped her hands on before hugging Sil and kissing his cheeks.

Sil immediately introduced us to his mother, Rena. Afterwards, she led us inside beneath a covering and beckoned us to sit down and eat. Rena spoke heartily, "I missed my boy. They didn't feed you well in that place. I have prepared a feast for you and your friends. All your favorite foods. Eat up, enjoy. Tonight you are home with your family."

The table was filled with all kinds of exotic fruits, breads and meats, and, I had to admit, it all looked appealing. All but the large whompas lying in the middle like a centerpiece. Before I could say no, Sil had already cut me a huge slice, and placed it on my plate.

He watched me anxiously, waiting for me to take a bite. Finally, I did, trying hard not to grimace. It wasn't too bad, though it still looked nasty. It was a large green, goober-faced fish, with black spots on its skin and small spiky fins. Celeste followed my lead and tasted it, too. She also seemed to think it was good enough to eat.

Rena made her way around to each of us, pouring on a thick, bubbly sauce which smelled like spinach and tasted the same. "Glad you like it," she said.

Nodding, I smiled gratefully and began cutting my whompas into small pieces. "Where are you headed, Déjà?" Peg inquired with interest.

"I'm glad you asked, because I was wondering if anyone knew how to get to Aruna?" I answered, hopefully. "I am on a quest to find my father, Octavius, and that is where he is. Do you know of it?"

Putting down his fork, Peg looked up and scratched under his chin. "Well, I'm not sure, but I think I might know. Aruna may well be about two or three doorways from here, depending on which one you enter. I recommend the door far to the east. Sil can take you tomorrow if you like. And you can drive the Wind Song, if you promise to be careful." Peg patted his son on the back.

Sil seemed pleased. "I will," he grinned. I guessed the Wind Song must be another spaceship.

"Do you know how to get there?" I questioned, sipping from a fruit cut in the shape of a bowl. "Where does the next door lead?"

"Don't worry. We'll have no problem finding it. The east doorway leads to the land of Kwata Calmoon. It's kind of dangerous, if you ask me. But if you must, I'll still take you."

"How dangerous? What do you mean?"

Peg cut in, breaking his bread, "There are strange creatures living there. They are like savages. You don't want to spend too much time in that place."

"Well, what about the other doorways?" I asked.

"There are doors on all four corners of the planet. North, South, East, and West. But the North and the South are impossible to get to. And unfortunately, the West leads back the way we came. Your best chance is to go to the East," Peg told me, wiping his face with a brown paper napkin.

"Well, I guess there is no other choice then," I agreed, staring at Sil to see what he'd say. He said nothing.

Sil was quite handsome and I noticed Celeste checking him out as she ate her food. But when I tapped her arm, she denied she was looking. In his own way, he reminded me of my own true love. I wondered what Joshua was up to. I wondered if he was visiting me at that very same moment.

I decided to retire early. Sil led me inside the trunk of the huge tree, to a neat little area carved near the nook. It was laden with a hanging hammock, rocking chair, and a tiny window from which one could see the best of the kingdom.

I stood at the window for a long while, staring silently out at the misty swamps. All around the habitat golden lamps were hung, glowing with fire. Whompas constantly buzzed around them, attracted to their blaze. Every now and then, the whompas would fly down and dip themselves in the water below. Refreshing, I'm sure. I could also hear the wildlife, making weird noises, deep in the darkness.

Settling down on the hammock, I pulled my father's journal from my backpack, and once again began to search for a fresh entry. The latest one read like this:

Mystic Deja: Maze Of Existence

Entry #60

    The yabosaurs and I have been traveling for a multitude of days. As we draw closer to Lake Tippitoin, my fears become greater. Thirteen of our crew have already perished from the poisonous sting of Antetnas which hide beneath the snow. Just one touch of its tail can cause everlasting sleep.

    Yesterday, a large geyser erupted, unleashing a towering column of hot water whirling our way. Since the tornado of steam soaked me, I have begun to get a little frostbitten. Tonight we will camp close to the forest. Hopefully, the silver assassins have not caught on to our whereabouts. Soon as I can, I will be on my way again. If you can make it here, I will see you shortly. Take care, my dear daughter — take care.

I didn't blame my father for being vexed. Great Reign was a threat that could keep him from waking. I knew I would have to face him sometime, if I hoped to bring Octavius back to reality. There was no evading the perilous encounter. He would not let us leave, because his existence depended on it.

    I had to be glad that I'd found a good ally, although I had

yet to finish my training. Zim Logi would understand. And I'd eventually go back to learn all his teachings. But first, I had to find Aruna, realm of ice where the yabosaurs lived.

The best thing for me was to stay up for the rest of the night and practice my emerging techniques. I hadn't forgotten the first of the lessons. I had plenty of time to practice it, too. Reminding myself, I started saying the formation, "Imagine, create, balance and control."

The room they gave me was cozy and exceptionally private. It was like living in a squirrel's den. The walls were cypress wood, and there was even a balcony by the window. I went out on the balcony and looked at the water. I could still see the three moons hovering above, like giant light bulbs illuminating the sky.

In the distance, I could see an endless forest of moss-covered cypress trees sticking up from the wet bottomland.

Suddenly, there was a knock at the door. "Come in," I said, and Celeste appeared, dressed in one of Rena's long dresses. She sat down in the rocking chair next to the hammock.

"What is it, Celeste? What's troubling you?" I asked. I could tell she had something on her mind, by the way she stared down at her feet.

"I've decided to stay here, with Sil," she answered shyly. She looked at me directly. "I want this to be my new home. I feel comfortable with them."

"Hey, that's great," I said. "You will be happy. And Sil is a nice guy. Smart, too."

"But what about you? You will be all alone. I'll be worried," she said.

"Don't worry about me, I am an Artisan, remember. Zim Logi will help me. Besides, I think Sil would miss you if you left."

Celeste sighed, and got up to look over the balcony. "You think so?" she said with a bit of eagerness.

"I'm sure of it."

Teasingly, I tapped her arm again, and made a deep grin. "I knew you liked him," I said, smiling.

Laughing, she replied, "He is pretty cute, huh?"

"Yep," I admitted.

Celeste had been given a cozy spot of her own, deep down at the bottom of the old cypress tree, close to the surface of the swampy water. It was prime pickings, because it was one of the largest rooms that they had carved out. And it was right down the hall, from Sil and his family.

Celeste went to the door and opened it to leave, putting her middle finger up to her mouth and biting her nail, briefly. I knew she was still concerned that I would get lost in the maze, and end up in trouble. So, I made one more attempt to put her mind at ease.

"My father is waiting for me," I said. "I'm looking forward to seeing him again. I bet he will be very easy to find."

"I'm sure you're right," she said optimistically. "Are you still going whompas fishing with us tomorrow, or do you intend to get an early start?"

"No, I'll wait till after our fishing trip. Might as well, since Sil is so excited."

"Okay, see you tomorrow then," she said as she exited.

I wasn't sure when I'd reach Aruna, or how far three doorways was, for that matter. But I was sure to make more good friends along the way.

Thirteen

The Rescuer's Chariot

That night I stayed awake and practiced my emerging. In the early morning, Sil asked me to meet him on the platform. Celeste was already there, looking excited about our fishing trip. I watched Sil pulling giant nets into a small starship which had the words "Wind Song" painted on its bottom left.

The Wind Song didn't seem like much of a ship because of its size, but Sil assured me it was fast and dependable.

The Hucki Muck swamplands were covered with a thick fog, and I couldn't see where we were going. Sil seemed to steer blindly around huge moss-covered trees, swerving in and around till he found a clearing that he claimed was the perfect spot.

He positioned the ship high above the wetland and docked it near a wooden balcony that encircled a tall cypress tree. "Help me with the nets," he said, as he pulled out a bulky knot of ropes. At first it all seemed complicated, spreading the net from one tree to another, but after we had completed the fastening, it all seemed to make sense.

"Will the whompas just fly into the net?" Celeste asked, staring up at the giant web.

"That's exactly what they'll do. Whompas have the worst vision, that's why they are attracted to brightness," Sil replied, turning on a huge white light.

"So now what do we do?" I asked.

"We just sit back, relax, and wait," Sil answered. "We can make a day of it."

We went up on the wooden balcony, eagerly awaiting our precious swarm to fly into our elaborate trap. I dangled my legs over the side while Celeste rested her back against the tree trunk. Sil did most of the watching. After the fog grew thin, the sun appeared, and the three of us lay back and daydreamed.

By late afternoon, the fog had turned to a gray mist. I grew hot and restless as the time went by. There had been no sight of any whompas fish, and I was beginning to believe we were wasting our time when, all of a sudden, I heard a nerve wracking sound.

Shaking Celeste, I stood up to see what it was. "I think I hear them coming," I exclaimed, almost leaping off the platform. "Sil," I yelled, "They're headed this way!" Holding onto the rails, I leaned over to get a better view.

Wiping his forehead, Sil came from the other side of the tree, and, squinting his eyes, looked out into the clearing. "Yeah, that's them all right. We'd better get ready. We'll have to pick them off and put them in this special container." Jumping on board the Wind Song, he disappeared, and emerged again, carrying a wooden cooler with a long tube protruding from its lid.

"You'd better be careful when you grab them," he stated.

"Why?" Celeste asked.

"Because they bite," Sil replied, chuckling to himself. "Trust me on this one."

The whompas came flying fast, diving down and taking a quick turn around a narrow tree. Then they flew up and headed straight for the bright light beam.

It happened consecutively, as one by one, the whompas got caught in our net. "This is almost too easy," Celeste grinned, reaching up to pull out one that was wiggling. "Ouch."

"What?" I asked.

"It bit me," she said, dropping the fish.

"I told you," said Sil, quickly scooping it up and pushing it through the extending cylinder mounted on top of the wooden cooler. "Pick them up by their tails."

Clumsily, I climbed onto the net and helped Sil as he pulled the whompas out from the crevices. I handed them down to Celeste who routinely stuffed them into the packing cooler. For a while, we busily worked ourselves into a sweat. When the work was done, and the packing cooler was full, Sil and Celeste carried it on board the Wind Song. I stood on the balcony and watched for more whompas.

Sitting down again, I sighed, and rested my head on the bark of the tree. But as I began to relax and enjoy the view, I noticed a flickering red light, coming from a distant branch. Quickly it moved from behind the leaves and headed in my direction. The closer it came, the more detail I could make out. I was stunned to see a small, mechanical robot.

It was broad, and had a huge lens for an eye. Once it drew near, I ducked down and peered under the rails, watching as it swung its lengthy legs over the net we had laid. It hovered for a few minutes, then disappeared into a grove of tree leaves.

"*Sil, I think you better come out here!*" I hollered.

"*What is it?*" he asked, hurrying to see what had me so excited.

"*Look,*" I said, pointing in the direction of the robot. It was now cruising our way again. I had caught its attention.

Celeste gasped as the robot drew near. "A silver probe," she exclaimed. "The silver assassins must be near."

"Uh, oh, we'd better get moving," Sil agreed. Another one appeared. This one was broadcasting a strange static noise, and vanished high above the trees.

By this time, adrenaline was pumping through my veins. The three of us fled hastily to the ship. Quickly, Sil got us moving. Once we were flying, I saw the trouble we were in.

A hundred or more androids were headed our way: not little robots like the kind we had just left, but enormous alien beings, flying in formation. They seemed like more than machines: a combination of life forms, with silvery hard skin and dark, hollow eyes.

"Faster Sil, they're gaining speed," Celeste squealed. She looked as if she might start to scream.

For a moment we sailed over an ocean of water. We were leaving the Hucki Muck swampland behind, and I knew we were headed for disaster.

Suddenly a ball—like a missile of fire—barely missed the ship; instead, it landed in the ocean, creating a tremendous splash. "Buckle up," Sil commanded. "If they hit us, we'll crash."

Obediently, Celeste and I buckled our seat belts; holding on to our arm rests as the ship started shaking. There was another splash, as another missile missed. The assassins were gaining speed, moving in like an army of bullets.

"Do we have any weapons?" I asked, knowing it would probably do no good. We were out-numbered, and our ship was too small. There was no time for a reply, the missiles kept coming, one after the other, until finally, we were struck and descended towards the body of water below. The Wind Song fell fast, and hit the ocean hard, knocking me around in my seat, and releasing my seat belt.

Instantly, the ship began to sink. Fortunately, none of us were really hurt as we scrambled through a hole that was rapidly taking in water. "Wait, you guys," I muttered in alarm. "I can't swim that well." I managed to float out. I was frightened, and began to panic.

I looked up into the sky as gigantic balls of fire flew toward me. Quickly I dived under the water holding my breath. My fears had become real, and I was sinking into the shadows, forgetting everything, as my mind darkened.

I don't remember exactly how long I floated there. It could have been minutes, seconds—all I know is that suddenly, I was being pulled into an airtight vacuum. It was a globe made of glass, like a princess' carriage. The moment I was inside, I started choking and gasping for air. Sil and Celeste were sleeping on the cushions. Instead of bothering to wake them, I turned to look around.

We were inside a plush dome carriage, still under water, and from what I could tell, being pulled by a pair of remarkably bony seahorses. The seahorses were not the average size for their species. They were quite hefty, and could compare to the dimensions of the horses back home.

While we were carried away in our rescuer's chariot, my mind raced back, wondering what had happened in the moments before we had been saved.

Fourteen
The Mysterious Coral Reef

My first thought was that perhaps someone had seen us and went to the trouble of coming to our rescue. But why hadn't they stayed to greet us? And where were we going?

I peered through the glass, looking for signs of a possible being. I could see all kinds of fish and life forms beneath the surface of the sea. It was such a beautiful sight that I soon settled down completely, and got comfortable in my seat.

I observed the seahorses as they propelled their dorsal fins repeatedly, steering us onward, towards our unknown destination. They camouflaged themselves well, changing from neutral beige to fluorescent orange and purple, keeping up with the scenery. Then the surroundings changed and we moved into a shallow coral reef.

It was no ordinary reef, but a landscape of erosion, rising from the sea. Our globular carriage began to slowly ascend until it floated on the face of the water, thus allowing us a perfect view of the isle.

Steadily, we moved down a marine ridge of calcium carbonate skeletons, brilliantly structured, I might add, and amazingly complex in form. Celeste and Sil awakened immediately, once the beams from the sun glared into their faces. We were all astonished and anxious, wondering who awaited in the coral dwellings.

Finally, the carriage came to a halt, and the globular glass top disappeared beneath the flooring. I jumped onto the reef, glancing around to see if someone was near. Sil and Celeste followed my lead.

"Hello," I called out, raising my eyebrows. But no one answered.

"Maybe they are waiting inside," Celeste suggested, pointing at an entryway that opened, invitingly.

"Maybe so," I said.

Smoothing her brown hair, Celeste headed for the opening. She was sure it would lead us to the rescuer's chambers. I, on the other hand, was a bit more cautious, and turned about repeatedly, trying to keep an eye out.

On the other side of the entry was a winding stairwell that

led downward, and into an area under the sea. In our exploration, we discovered sleeping quarters with a most unique view of the coral ecosystem, an empty chamber, except for a pedestal that held up a seahorse-shaped bracelet, and a locked door, that we couldn't get open. Aside from that, there was a gallery of seahorse paintings, and to my surprise, several unicorn statues in various parts of the residence. But still, no sign of the mysterious rescuer.

In the back of my mind, there was something faintly familiar about this place. But I couldn't quite put my finger on it yet.

Momentarily, I shivered.

"What?" Sil asked, still trying the locked door.

"Nothing, just déjà vu," I said, as I stared at the artsy carvings in the coral.

Suddenly, an unfamiliar voice came from the other side of the room. "Only one person can open that," it screeched.

The three of us immediately turned to see who spoke, and were much surprised to find a red-tailed, black cockatoo, sitting on a perch.

"And who might that be?" I asked, creeping slowly toward the bird.

"Well, *you*, of course," it said frankly, picking its wings and blinking its eyes.

"*Me*, what do you mean, *me*?" I questioned, doubting it was telling the truth.

"*You* are the one, Miss Déjà, yes *you*," it replied, this time ruffling its wing a little, seeming to be a little irritated.

"Why me? Where is the owner of this domain?" I asked with a look of puzzlement.

"*You* are the owner of this domain. Yes *you*, yes *you*," the cockatoo repeated.

"I don't believe you," I said sternly. Sil and Celeste were staring at each other.

"*Open* it and see, Miss Déjà, yes *open* it," it dared.

Promptly, I went over to the door and turned the knob. When the door actually opened, I could not believe what I found inside. It was full of clothes. But the startling part was they were all my style of fashions. There were maxi coats made of fine materials and patterns, thick-heeled boots in various lengths, and hats, lots of historical hats, including my favorite top hat, arrayed in short and tall heights.

"Told you so. Told you so," the bird cracked, loudly.

Celeste immediately reached for a military hat from the 1940s. "Neat stuff," she chuckled, trying it on.

"But where did it come from?" I asked.

"You must have created it, unknowingly," Sil said. "You know, with your emergy."

"But shouldn't I know, when I create something?" I said

staring at the various coat jackets. Now I was preoccupied, trying to figure things out. I didn't remember creating any of it. I thought back and shook my head.

"Couldn't it have happened when you almost drowned?" Celeste guessed.

"I suppose so," I said. "Come to think of it, I do remember dreaming, about seahorses."

"Well, that's it then," she replied, picking a Mexican sombrero from the shelf.

"But this isn't right," I said. "I shouldn't be materializing things without planning them out. What if something goes wrong?"

"Don't worry so much," said Sil. "You saved us, didn't you? I think I'll have another look at that bracelet." He narrowed his eyes and went into the gallery.

Still having doubts about what really happened, I tentatively accepted their reasoning, and went off to do some exploring, leaving Celeste alone with the Cockatoo and the closet full of clothes. I had a great desire to introduce myself to those wonderful seahorses that helped us escape.

I took a deep breath and went to the entrance from whence we came. The carriage bobbed quietly near the edge of the coral, and the seahorses were sleeping softly, still attached to their reins. Bending down, I reached into the crystal blue water and touched one of the bony fish on the right side of its snout. Lifting its head slightly above the water, the sea creature leaned into my stroking and gave me a warm look.

Leaning further in, I patted the second one on its glistening wet skin, smiling to show my appreciation. "Thank you for saving us," I said, gazing into their big, bubbly eyes. Both seahorses nodded and seemed to understand completely.

Beyond the majestic carriage, a twinkling of light caught my attention. Blinking heavily, I watched as Zim Logi appeared. I froze for a second as he serenely drifted over the water, moving gracefully towards me.

"Where have you been?" I bellowed sharply. "I've been having a hard time since I last saw you." He had not changed in his appearance. He still wore the same fancy smile and the long cerulean robe.

"I can see you've learned a great many things," Zim Logi replied, reaching over and touching a seahorse's snout. He turned to me and grinned.

"Can you believe it? I made all of this," I said.

"And you grow stronger too, the more you imagine. Soon you will not know your own creativity."

"You mean, I am creating more and more of this illusion, as well as my father?"

"Actually, yes. You are generating your own realms of existence, without even knowing it." I realized how far I'd come, without even practicing.

Zim Logi's smile faded quickly and was replaced by a more serious pose.

"I've come to tell you that you must leave at once," he said.

"Now?" I bitterly responded, not ready to leave.

"There is great danger here. The assassins are still searching for you. You pose a serious threat to the Great Reign's plans to control your father."

"But what about my new domain? I can't just leave everything. What if they find it?" I asked, directing his attention to the two seahorses.

"I will teach you to hide it deep within you, like I do with mine. Come on, you can make it invisible. We must hurry."

"No, I must take it with me," I insisted.

"If you must," said Logi.

"Wait!" I gasped. Sil and Celeste are still inside. Shouldn't they be away from here when I do this?"

"Of course," said Zim Logi raising his eyebrows. "You must take me to them."

I nodded fervently and led him to the gallery where Sil had gone to inspect the bracelet. He and Celeste were standing there when we entered. They turned to look at us with increasing curiosity.

"This is Zim Logi," I said. "He says I have to go before the assassins get here. There will be two new seahorses waiting to take you back to the Hucki Muck swamplands. You must leave here at once. There isn't much time."

Sil moved towards me and stared deeply into my eyes. He pulled me to the side. "Can you make it alone?" he whispered.

"Yes, I'm sure I will be alright. I have more than a guide," I said, turning towards my teacher.

"But the east door is too far away. You need me to show you," he stated. He seemed to want to go with me.

"Don't worry. My father is waiting," I told him. "You have to go, so I can make sure nobody else can come here."

"The door is already here," Zim Logi put in. "It will become visible when she has completed her task."

With much hesitance, Sil gave in, and after placing the bracelet he was holding, in my hand, he hugged me goodbye. Instantly, I remembered that the bracelet was made for a reason. I was certain that if I put it on, I would know why I had crafted it.

The silver bracelet had a seahorse molding, and it wrapped its tail around my wrist the moment it was secured. Unexpectedly, one of the ringlets, the very last, released itself and fell to the floor.

"Give me your hand, Sil," I insisted, finally understanding what I was supposed to do with it. He gave me a searching look. I reached down and picked up the ringlet. "This is a calling device," I said, watching it twine around his wrist. "If I need you, I can call by pressing my fingers here between the ringlets like this, I showed them. Then travel will be instant, but not permanent, so you'll be able to get back home."

Pausing, I gazed smartly at Celeste and motioned her closer. "This one's for you," I said automatically, releasing another to secure itself around her arm.

"I will miss you," she said, and hugged me gently. "You promise to be careful."

"I will," I said. "Now you two get going." Zim Logi was giving me an anxious look.

As the both of them retreated towards their rides, Zim Logi stood facing me. "You will have to concentrate, and disorganize the dimensions. But you must be careful not to disrupt the balance. Remember what happened during practice last time."

Reaching back with my mind, I recalled my performance and how the water put out the fire, and the wind blew away the dust, leaving nothing. I knew, though, that this time it would be different. I was more confident, and less ambivalent.

When I was sure my friends were a distance away, I concentrated on my imagining with all my emergy, forcing the scenery to fold up into swirling images. "Modify the dimensions," Zim Logi bellowed through the commotion.

As I focused, I felt myself lifting slightly from the ground. The room around me spun faster and faster, till it was a blur of imagery. I had made a whirlpool of pictures that engulfed their surroundings, including part of the corals beneath us. Like a huge tidal wave, I kept pushing it downward, dividing the water from the bottom of the ocean's floor, revealing the doorway, and the hairy beast that kept it.

I took a deep breath, gathering all the remaining pieces. The images receded into the palm of my hand making the shape of a small glass marble, which I quickly sealed in the mouth of the bracelet. As the wall of seawater spun, Zim Logi and I moved towards the doorway. "Will you be coming with me?" I asked.

"No, but I'll be around when you need me," he said, staring into the Door Keeper's hypnotic eyes. This one was nothing like the first. Instead of being sleepy, it was wide awake and had an unkempt velvet coat.

"You may ask the Keeper a question," Zim Logi said.

"May I enter the doorway, please?" I asked the waving, carpet creature.

"Yes you may," the Door Keeper replied. "You are already there."

Fifteen

Koala Corner

The new realm was hot and hazy. The sun seemed too close for comfort and I had to squint just to see where I was going. I gazed around at the unfamiliar region.

I could tell I was in some sort of thick, eucalyptus-filled jungle. There were many tall gum trees blocking my view. I looked up at the gray tree that was closest to me. The light bounced through the leaves revealing a clump of gray fur.

I gasped.

Huddled close together was a family of koalas, hugging each other on the tip of a branch. "It's me, *Coconut*," I heard a voice say in my head.

"*Coconut,* is that you up there?" I said aloud. "*How did you get here?*"

"I wanted to come with you," the voice replied. It was as if I was the only one that could hear him.

"But *how, how* did you get here?" I asked again. Scratching my forehead, I began to think about the plausible explanations. Not only did I suspect Coconut had somehow joined in on my illusions, but I was also sure he was actually taking part in the creations.

There was a moment of silence. I could not figure it out.

Sighing, I envisioned my beloved backpack, and instantly it appeared on my shoulder. I dug into the bag until I found the binoculars and put them to my eyes, so I could get a better look.

"*Wow!*" I murmured. I had not noticed it before, but there was a colony of koalas relaxing in the scene. They were everywhere.

"Déjà…Déjà…" I heard the voice in my head again.

"You never answered my question," I hollered. Coconut was making his way down the tree towards me. He stopped for a moment and sniffed the air passionately.

"I am connected to you somehow. I believe you are reading my mind, listening to my inner thoughts," he said.

For a moment I was skeptical. I wondered if I had somehow developed mental telepathy. Zim Logi did say that my creativity would become stronger the longer I remained

KOALA CORNER

entranced. Well, what else could it be? "Are you asleep back in your habitat at home?" I shouted.

"What do you think koalas do all day?" he said sharply. "And you don't have to shout, you know. I can hear you just the same."

I had the sudden impulse to check my belt timer. When I saw that it read 1 hour and 20 minutes, I felt calmer. I was tired and sleepy and wanted to see Joshua. It felt like I had been away from him forever.

Coconut leaned over me, still clinging to the tree with his sharp claws, in the most awkward position. I sat down on the ground at the base of the trunk, and scrounged through the backpack for items. I picked up a ripened peach, and after I had taken a bite of it, I pulled out the journal and started looking for a new entry.

Entry #61

We have finally reached the icy glaciers of the Timoe Dali. It comforts me to know that you are not far from me. The next door, perhaps, will bring us together again. The yabosaurs have trained me to protect myself from the shapeshifters, dwellers of the underground. Getting past them will be the hardest part of our journey. I have heard they are highly intelligent and

> telepathic beings that do not like trespassers. But there is no other way. I must get to the next realm if I am to ever see Jenasee again.
>
> Great Reign has sent out silver probes to every sphere in search of my whereabouts. You must be careful, too. There is no telling how far he will go to find us. Once you get to Aruna, the yabosaurs will help you make it safely to the Timoe Dali. They have already been alerted that you are coming and are awaiting your arrival. Good luck and see you soon.

By the time I finished reading I knew I had no time to lose. Octavius would be reaching the next doorway soon, and I needed to be there before he leapt through it. There was no telling where he'd end up, or how long it would take me to find him. I stood up and dusted myself off.

From the corner of my eye, I saw something. My senses told me I was in grave danger. I felt as if an evil presence was moving in closer to where I was standing.

Looking up the tree, I shrieked, "*Coconut, we've got to go!*" Coconut had climbed to the top and was sleeping quietly. He turned his neck towards me and looked down. I heard a bustle of leaves somewhere in the distance. That weird feeling grew stronger.

"Come on," I called. "We've got to go." A noise rang out like a chorus of hunger, creating a domino effect of fear. All of the koalas seemed to magically disappear into the forest. After a few minutes, Coconut and I were the only ones left. Coconut sat with his ears sticking out, straining to listen, scared stiff.

Grrrrrrrrgguhh! There it was again. "*Now!*" I said urgently. Holding the knapsack open, I motioned for him to jump. I was definitely scared. That sound was so nasty, it reminded me of the hairy Troluk man-eaters.

I couldn't see anything, but I could hear. I could feel it getting closer and closer. *Wait*, my instincts were telling me. There were more than one.

I heard branches crackling and bushes being whisked in the wind. "*Jump!*" I said in sheer terror. It was moving fast. Coconut obeyed. Once in the knapsack, he dug down, trying to hide himself under my father's journal and the KRAMM computer.

I spun around. What I saw would make even a heavyweight flinch. They were monsters, creatures of doom; two legged beasts with bulging chests, angry eyes and sharp, mad dog teeth. Each one had a wide, twisted, crazy court jester face, long twitching arms and small buttocks. How many were there I could not tell, for they were coming from the shadows, out from behind trees and bushes, like a pack of wolves homing in for the kill.

They sped towards us. I took off running. I raced, backpack knocking against my shoulders, scattering twigs and splashing through puddles of rainwater. There was no place to hide.

I kept my pace, but I felt them gaining on us. I could actually see a dark brown blur of a shape running along side of me. At any moment, it could just reach out with its long arms and grab me by the throat.

"Hang on!" I said, grabbing a hold of a swinging vine and kicking off the side of a tree. In two short shakes I was sailing through the air, grabbing at anything I could use to thrust me as far away as possible. Coconut hung tightly to my neck, almost squeezing my breath away.

I reached a strong twig and decided to wait it out. Squatting low, I checked to see if the beasts were still following us.

"Look what you've gotten us into," I fussed. "Where's the exit?"

"How should I know," he said grumpily.

"You are the one having this nightmare," I scolded. "Shhh. Here they come!"

We watched silently as the "creature feature" passed swiftly underneath us. As they disappeared through the woods, I started thinking about the KRAMM com. I thought maybe I could get some answers about the display of ugliness I had just witnessed.

I held out my hands and the small computer emerged immediately. "Let's just stay up here for a while," I said, typing in the description. I waited a second after hitting the enter key, until an image of our attacker appeared on the short screen.

The report said:

> **GANGOBY**
>
> FOUND ONLY ON THE SKYLAND OF KWATA CALMOON, GANGOBIES ARE DANGEROUS BEASTS THAT LIKE THE SKILL OF THE HUNT. USUALLY THEY DWELL IN NUMBERS RANGING FROM 20 TO 50 AND FOLLOW A LEADER WHO HAS A DISTINGUISHING MARK ON HIS CHEST. GANGOBIES MAY DESTROY THEIR PREY JUST FOR FUN, LEAVING THE CARCASS BEHIND FOR DEVOURING LATER. THEY ARE CARNIVORES AND KEEP MOSTLY TO THEMSELVES UNTIL THEY ARE HUNGRY.
>
> THESE HIGHLY SKILLED HUNTERS CANNOT BE FOOLED. THEY HAVE AN EXCELLENT SENSE OF SMELL AND CAN LOCATE A PREY IN HIDING UP TO 10 MILES AWAY. NEVER UNDERESTIMATE THEIR SEARCHING TECHNIQUES. YOU WILL FIND THAT THE ONLY WAY TO GET RID OF THEM IS TO SHAPESHIFT. THAT WILL THROW

**THEM OFF TRACK. OTHERWISE, AMMUNI-
TION AND TAKING FLIGHT IS THE ONLY
CHANCE OF A POSSIBLE ESCAPE.**

"Great, Coconut, we are on a skyland," I whispered. *"There is no exit."* Thinking for a moment, I decided to type in Kwata Calmoon for more information. The only thing else helpful was the fact that the skyland was just above another realm called Caltoss. It was supposed to be sandy and deserted, but had four doorways.

I set my mind to figuring out how we were going to get there. I still couldn't help wondering if the Gangobies were somewhere around, waiting for us to climb down from the tree, so they could snatch us up and tear us to pieces.

According to the KRAMM com, we were not too far from the edge of the skyland. All we had to do was find a good spot where I could create a flying machine. At this point, the jetwing hover-bike would do fine.

Cautiously, I lowered myself down from the tree, Coconut secured in my backpack. I began running in the direction that the KRAMM com said the edge of the skyland was located. Hopefully, there would be a big enough clearing to do my mind work.

The coast seemed clear. I tore through the jungle, never once looking back. As I sped towards the edge, a foul smell seeped into the air, filling my nostrils with a rotten stench of dead meat. I slowed down a little to catch my breath. I reached an area that looked just wide enough for me to place the hover-bike. Turning around, I did a 360, surveying the scene to make sure it was safe.

After a moment, I focused my mind on the hover-bike's details, until it materialized completely in the center of the grassy plain. Coconut must have sent me a telepathic message because, all of a sudden, I felt tense.

Grrrrrrrgguhhh! Closing my eyes briefly allowed me to see through his. I felt as if my heart was going to leap out of my chest. "A *Gangoby*," I thought to Coconut. *"Don't move."* The Gangoby was huge, bigger than all the others. He had a strange mark that distinguished him as the one in charge.

I must have looked like a crazy fool, standing there frozen,

with a Gangoby drooling down the back of my neck. His razor sharp teeth were only inches away from Coconut's face. And I was sure that if I made a sudden move, he would instantly devour him.

While I was contemplating my next step, several of the gangobies came into view. I realized that we were surrounded. They had probably been following us the whole time.

The hover-bike was ready but I was too scared to jump on. The seconds ticked by, while the gangobies moved nearer.

"Transform, *shapeshift*. Please do *something*," Coconut blasted into my head.

"If I only knew how," I replied, making a fist, gearing myself up for a fight.

"It's just like changing clothes," he said. "It's the same principle."

"How did you get to be so smart?" I said, raising my eyebrows. "*Never mind.*"

Coconut was right, because it wasn't as hard as I thought it would be. All I did was imagine it clearly, and Coconut and I had instantly started changing. As our faces shifted, it felt like a bad headache. Soon, the rest of our bodies shifted as well, turning into a replicated gangoby. Coconut and I had merged into one.

The leader of the pack even stopped his growling, giving us a look of pure astonishment. I took it as a sign that they were distracted, and crept over to the hover-bike. As I mounted the bike, I glanced back and saw the head gangoby staring inquisitively.

Slowly, the hover-bike lifted off the ground, leaving the gangobies dazed and confused. Once we were safely away, Coconut and I instantly changed back to ourselves, both of us sighing with relief.

Once again, I wore a bomber jacket and goggles. Coconut wore his own cute jacket and goggles that I created to match. His neck scarf waved rapidly in the wind as we soared through the clouds just out of reach of the angry gangobies.

Glancing up underneath the skyland made me shiver. It cast a shadow the size of a mountain. For now, I felt happy, even thrilled that our escape went so well. Coconut kept me company, and that alone was an added pleasure.

It was a long way down. But the best thing of all was I felt my father getting nearer. I had a sneaking suspicion that the very next doorway was the one place I had been searching for: Aruna. And I would be there soon if I just kept heading in the right direction.

I had a big smile on my face as we went flying into a fluffy cloud. I couldn't see anything except mist. Slowly everything became clear again.

Sixteen
Mental Reign

My 1 hour and 20 minutes were up. Still I stood in the stasis chamber, clutching the air of the imaginary handle bars trying to get a grip on reality. The hatch swung open and the familiar sounds and smells of home came rushing in, waking me completely out of my mesmeric state.

Professor Onyx was watching me as I cautiously made my way to the bottom of the stairwell. "Déjà," he asked, "Any new updates? How is it coming?"

I glanced at him, disoriented, and said, "I'm getting closer for sure. I'm certain I'll see him soon." All of sudden my stomach was growling for food and water, my muscles ached a little when I walked, and my head felt like a brick was banging up against the inside of my skull. Miss Hawthorne helped me out of my uniform.

"*Excuse me*, I have to go to the …" I muttered. For a minute, I felt like throwing up. The transition from hallucination to actuality was too sudden. My mind had no time to catch up with my body. As I bolted from the room, I could hear the Professor saying, "I think she was in too long this time. We need to keep it at a maximum of 12."

Instead of throwing up, I wound up in the kitchen fixing myself a plate full of snacks. I took an aspirin and headed for my bedroom with all the goodies. As soon as I was settled down, I picked up the telephone and dialed Joshua's number.

"Hey there Boo, what ya doing?" I said, as soon as I heard his manly voice.

"Nothing much, what about you?" he answered. It was half past 8 pm and I was ready to fill him in on all the details.

"Guess what?" we both said at the same time. "What?" I hastily put in.

"Naw, you go first," he insisted.

"No, why don't you, because I am eating anyway?" I said, picking up a chicken salad sandwich, sniffing the bread.

"Well, I went to an audition today."

"Really?" I asked, trying not to smack. "What kind of audition? And why didn't you mention it before?"

"I just found out about it at the last minute. It was only a couple of guys who are trying to start a band," he said. "They want me to play the guitar."

"That's good. How did you do?"

"I think I did pretty well. When I got there I was real nervous, but after I met everybody, I started feeling relaxed. This one guy, named Diego, seemed kind of old school. He could play though. He and I both are big fans of Jimi Hendrix." He went on for a while. Then he said, "Hey, you want to hear this new jam?"

I could hear him plucking the strings intensely, making a rhythmic, funky sound, but it was fading away like a sweet lullaby, as I soon drifted off to sleep.

As I slept, I felt the tension in my brain ease away, and for a good while everything was serene. Then my mind started to race. I dreamt about the notorious "Heart Tickler". He was leaning over Octavius, about to cut him with an electric blade. He stopped for a moment and looked up at me, cold eyes bulging, metallic teeth dripping with blood. I screamed, and then the blade turned a bright fluorescent hue.

I was still screaming when I came to, and realized what I was really staring at. I looked across the room at my maxi coat pocket. The phone was still off the hook, so I picked it up, listened, then hung it up.

The bedroom was dim, and extraordinarily chilly. The window was closed, but a cool breeze crawled up my night gown. As I started toward the hanging coat, I suddenly felt an overwhelming sense of anxiety. For some odd reason, I knew that what I was about to discover would change my life forever.

"*No way,*" I said to myself, pulling out the tiny mushrooms. "*This isn't real.*"

I remembered picking them in the cave before I was chased by the swarm of angry glow bugs. Surely, I was hallucinating. Or was I? It seemed to be real.

I remembered what my uncle had said about the sole receptacle changing me. I was afraid that something weird would happen, and quickly resolved not to tell anyone.

I made a frantic dash out the bedroom after pulling on my jumpsuit and boots. Remnants of the recent nightmare reminded me that my father's life was still at stake.

The secret room was deserted except for my father's stasis chamber. Uncle Onyx and Miss Hawthorne had probably retired to their quarters, giving me time without their supervision.

What I needed to do was see his face, assure myself that he was alive. And when I reached him, I tried not to become unnerved. It was clear to me he was still breathing. However, his body looked stiff, as if his life force was draining with each breath.

Suiting up, I touched the glass lid of the stasis chamber with my two middle fingers, and then switched on the computer that hooked to the receptacle. I put in 24 hours, knowing there could be consequences, and hurried up the stairs to the specially made chamber.

The minute I was back in, it was as if I had never been gone. Coconut was clinging tightly to my shoulders while craning his neck to see the sand dunes below.

"Hold on!" I shouted, as the hover-bike hit the ground, bouncing a few paces before it came to a halt. Holding out my hands, I materialized the binoculars, stood up, and searched the perimeters for any kind of landmark. I needed something to input into the KRAMM com. The climate was dry and dusty like the deserts of Egypt.

"You see anything?" Coconut telepathically communicated, chewing on the eucalyptus leaves he had taken from a tree on Kwata Calmoon.

"No, I don't. And did you know you were heavy?" I sarcastically replied. He ignored me and kept nibbling.

"You stay here for a minute while I have a look around."

Carefully, I pulled off my backpack and placed it neatly on the seat of the hover-bike. Coconut crawled out, still gnawing at his food.

I sighed. The soil that surrounded me was a soft spread of baking hot sand. Fearful of losing time, I walked out a ways, continually checking the binoculars for any structures or life signs.

"Nothing. I didn't see a thing," I told Coconut after I had returned to the hover-bike. "Wonder which direction we should go in?"

Reaching into the backpack, I pulled out the KRAMM com and typed in Aruna. The computer said, "No data found."

Kicking up a pile of dust, I frowned at Coconut and muttered, "Man, I should've added more information last night. It might take us forever to find the next door."

"What's that?" Coconut communicated mentally. He sat up straight, and sniffed the air.

I could hear it, too. It was like loud thunder. The ground began to shake. I grabbed the binoculars and put them to my eyes. In the distance, I could faintly see a dark cloud forming at the horizon. It was blurry at first, but as I focused the lens, I began to distinguish more clearly.

"*Silver assassins!*" I shrieked. "WHAT….HOW did they find me?" I jumped onto the bike, and quickly shoved Coconut into the backpack. After it was secured to my shoulders, I started the engine and sped off.

Coconut and I were zooming over the terrain, building up a trail of smoke and soot behind us. I could feel the evil army gaining, ready to make war. Mysteriously, they were moving at the speed of light. Instantly, they had outrun the hover-bike, and created a barricade in front of me, blocking my route.

The wall they formed came up so suddenly I had no time to maneuver. I tried to turn quickly, to avoid a collision, instead causing the bike to flip over and out of control. The backpack and Coconut landed a few feet away from where I struck the ground. Quickly, I jumped to my feet, ready to protect myself from whatever the assassins might try to expel.

Instead, the ground beneath me began to split open until

it had cut a complete ring, 50 feet in circumference around where I stood. It began to rise, shooting rapidly into the sky. Abruptly, it stopped a mile up. It was at that moment, I distorted my wardrobe back to the original black, maxi-coat outfit.

As I regained my fighting position, I heard a loud voice say, "Release your emergy!" It was a strange and hypnotic tone, and I was almost forced to obey, until I caught sight of the being from which it was coming.

He came forth out of nowhere, cloaked in a long silver and black robe, much like Zim Logi's. His mouth and nose, however, were covered by a black cloth, exposing only his alluring and dynamic eyes. He wore a silver helmet with a pointed tip. It had a sharp spiky blade running down the back center. His eyes were dark as coals, showing a galaxy reflection that revealed his ancient age.

I knew without knowing, who he was. No one else could be him.

"GREAT REIGN," I said breathlessly. He silently stared.

"*Release your emergy or you will die!*" he hissed, suddenly emerging a troop of silver assassins my way. I returned a dark look, even though I was surrounded. In the next instant I pressed my fingers against my calling device.

Immediately, Sil and Celeste appeared, both bewildered by the sudden teleportation. Before they could speak a syllable I screeched, "*Brace yourself!*" and nodded my head towards the invaders.

We were all three facing our enemies, backs to each other, in the middle of the highland that Great Reign had sprung from the floor of the ground. There was always the chance that either of us could go sprawling off the side of it at the slightest toss from the assassin's assault. But none of us were fearful. They both had me, and I had them. We were a team.

There was a mad rush, and suddenly, legs kicked, bodies spun, and assassins came forth like a gang of ninjas with bad attitudes. I reached back and punched an assassin in the stomach, watching in wonder as my arm sunk inward, and he slowly disintegrated.

Great Reign must be controlling them all at the same time, I thought. That's why they are such unstable creations. I reasoned that if he controlled only one or two, they would be unstoppable. I would have to turn my attention on him in order to succeed.

There were too many silver assassins. Some were ascending from the depths below, climbing up the earth tower at an alarming pace. As soon as we had fought off one set, another one sprung over the sides. I blinked hard, staring into those mindless green eyes.

I spun toward Great Reign, kicking him hard in the face, but he was quick, and before I could strike, he threw me back. I let out an angry cry as I flew over the side and landed on another rising, towering terrain. Great Reign leaped forward and joined me on top of it.

Suddenly, the scenery altered. It was just him and me in the center of a vast universe, still standing on the terrain. Black stars twinkled harmoniously around, and the wind blew fiercely against my sunburned skin.

Again, the backdrop startled me. He was creating, and recreating again. I stood still, but the environment moved, changing at his will. This time I saw a silver city. His domain. The Great Metropolis, that was the center of the universe. All the technology encompassed the void, filling it with his hideous advancements.

I could only shudder at what I saw—heaving mechanisms of mass destruction, flying creatures with curious tasks, like the giant robot that seemed to be constantly building.

"Release your emergy. Do not try to fight it," he said. "There is someone else I wish to conquer."

I could see he was using me as bait. And I knew who he was really after. Angrily I emerged a ball of fire, hurling it furiously towards him. "*I will never let you take him!* FIGHT ME!," I yelled.

I could feel the weight of the counter-attack as he emerged a large, silver shield, blocking flames before they could sear him. We were some distance apart, in a time warp, which formed our actions into broken-down motions. I watched him quickly emerge from his mind, a mechanical reptile the size of a dragon. But it was partly machine and I knew it had the same weakness as the assassins did.

Stumbling back, I ducked down. In another moment I emerged an organic replica—a celestial being, and while I was at it, I distorted the panorama to the view of the sea.

The two creatures fought violently, tails wrapping around, tearing into one another, until they had vanished, squealing, into the watery depths below.

Great Reign was quick. He moved with lightning speed, altering the landscape once more, giving it an expanse of continuous spiky blades. Then with a huge shake, the terrain I was standing on began to crumble. He was disarming. I was diminishing.

Swiftly, I broke his emerging concentration, and split open the void, bringing us back to Caltoss where I saw the fighting continued. I wondered how they could have lasted all this time. Great Reign had focused all his attention on me.

But now he was in full command again. Before I could stop him, he started using his power to control the assassins. Sil and Celeste were being encased in a clear cube that was quickly filling with a watery liquid.

"Release your emergy, or your friends will perish," Great Reign demanded.

"NO!" Celeste furiously yelled. "Don't let him take it! You will become his *slave*."

I watched, wide-eyed, as the prisms became half full. My friends banged against the glass, trying to break free of the restraint, before they suffocated and drowned. I could not stand it any longer.

I was becoming weak, losing control. My forehead began to tingle. I could feel him invading my mind. He was capturing my most precious gift, and I did nothing to stop him. Slowly the incandescent light particles began to leap forth, swirling synchronously.

As I fell to my knees, I could barely hear anything, but then, gradually, Zim Logi appeared. With a quickness he encased Great Reign into a block of ice and brought back my emergy.

As long as Great Reign remained encompassed, the silver assassins were gone. Zim Logi swiftly released Sil and Celeste from their coffins. I glanced over at Great Reign. He had broken free of the prison, and was seething with rage.

Noticing that his silver troops had vanished, he said sharply, "You shall not escape *me!*" Then he turned towards Zim Logi and hissed, "*Watch your back!*"

Gradually, he faded away. He'd return, though. I was sure of it. He had not completely been defeated, just thrown off guard by Zim Logi's reappearance. Maybe he would have to rethink his plans. Whatever he did, I was glad he was gone.

"What a fight," I finally choked out. I was standing next to my friends panting, while Zim Logi made the ground level again.

"Celeste sighed with relief. "We were almost dead meat," she whispered weakly.

"Almost," I said thankfully, patting Sil and Celeste on the shoulders.

"We were lucky this time," Zim Logi said, knowingly. "But all of you fought well. And you, Déjà, were especially creative." I stood there remembering.

"Glad we could help," Sil chuckled, rubbing his bruised chin.

"Next time, call us before it gets too far," Celeste said. All three of us laughed, except Zim Logi. He seemed to be in deep meditative thought.

"How does he move in and out of thin air?" I asked him, disrupting his state of contemplation.

"Only an Emergist can move through time and space," he

said. "It comes with much skill and control. It is the highest level of your training."

"About my training, I—"

He cut me off abruptly, "Never mind now. You must not waste time. Your father leaves through the next doorway soon. I will contact you again when you are ready."

As the ground reformed, I darted over to where Coconut was sitting and picked him up.

"You all right?" I asked, checking his limbs for broken bones. He seemed to be fine.

"I'm all right—they didn't harm me," he telepathically said, bracing his arms around my neck as I carried him. Sil helped me gather my things and put them back into the backpack. Zim Logi had somehow disappeared without so much as a hint of goodbye.

After saying our farewells, Sil and Celeste were teleported back home.

As I managed to thrust the heavy hover-bike horizontal again, I saw Zim Logi fade into being.

"You don't need the craft. I will take you to the next doorway. Just give me your hand," he said.

The moment I reached out to him, the atmosphere folded.

Seventeen

Make Ready Your Mind

A new wooly beast hovered aimlessly before me. His wiry hair glistened and moved with the air currents. He was a super-white-colored brute with small sparkling shimmers laden in his fur. The gruff face he carried led me to believe he was one to be reckoned with. Coconut was afraid and retreated into my backpack, covering his face underneath the flip-flap.

The creature grinned roughly, revealing pearly white teeth that were lined up almost flawlessly straight. "Tell me, Zim Logi, about the Door Keepers?" I said, "Where do they come from?"

Zim Logi smiled at me as if he was remembering something distant. He looked deep into the Door Keeper's large gray eyes and the carpet creature returned the expression. Okay, they were sharing a moment. But I wanted to know what the big secret was about.

"*A long time ago*, all Emergists kept watch over one realm of existence. But soon new dominions were created and our universe expanded. During this time, there was still a sense of peace. Then one highly skilled Emergist, called Zahra Alain, decided he wanted to reign over them all. He sought to generate and fill this empty void with infinite plains of limitless technology. That was the beginning of chaos. He kept traveling the realms, dividing them into regions. He quickly reached the verge of having full reigning power.

From that time on, the ancient Emergists that created the realms were at war with him. They soon saw that there was no way to conquer him. At this time we came together to choose a different form of protection."

"Hmm..." I said, "This is very interesting..."

"The Door Keepers were created to keep guard, so that each realm would stay separated. However, there was a fierce battle, and all the Emergists were forced to go into hiding. This left the old realms at the mercy of the Great Reign. The Door Keepers, however, still keep their watch, and cannot be removed unless all the remaining Emergists give up their emergies," Zim Logi remembered.

Make Ready Your Mind

"So you can not undo what another Emergist has designed?" I asked, staring at the huge entry that floated above the sand. "This explains why Great Reign needs so badly to control all the emergies."

"Yes, Déjà, you are correct," Zim Logi nodded.

"Is that why you have been away for over 500 years?" I asked. "So there are other Emergists like you, hiding out as fugitives? Surely, if every one put their minds together, they should be able to figure out a way to defeat him."

"Maybe, but the time is not yet," he said.

I knew he was getting anxious again and wanted me to focus on my mission. He did not like to talk.

Turning my attention towards the Keeper I asked, "How do I get to the other side?"

The Keeper said, "You are *already* there."

Giving Zim Logi a quick look of adieu, I watched as the new atmosphere twirled and danced, making a spectacle of itself, before heaving a sigh and resting on a pristine picture.

Coconut came out from under the flip-flap shaking. I, too, was quivering at the sudden gust of cold weather that stirred the blankets of snow.

"ARUNA!" I yelled, jumping at what I saw. And so it was.

Leaving the Door Keeper at the entrance, I walked towards the horizon. It was a backdrop of snowy mountains, cliffs and valleys, as well as a few lakes and massive pine trees.

"I don't like the cold," Coconut muttered mentally.

Instantly, I changed our attire. We couldn't get much further in this chilly climate without a new white coat with a much-needed hood.

"You happy now?" I asked, ready to explore.

"Not really. I don't think a coat is going to help all that much," he complained.

"Stop fussing," I said, "You can always go home."

"Never mind," he exclaimed, pulling the hood over his head.

Straightening the backpack to fit snuggly, and balancing out the load, I trudged through the snow, making my way towards the mountains. As I took slow, heavy steps, I noticed the milky terrain begin to shift.

"Be *careful*, you could be going in *one* direction and end up in *another*," I could hear myself saying over and over as I fell. It was Professor Onyx's warning that I should be watchful about the double reception.

Drenched from head to toe in icy cold water, I climbed out of the crystal blue river and glanced around at my koala. He and the backpack had fallen off on the way down. When I found him I was thankful that he had not been hurt, for all of a sudden we had dropped a disturbing distance from where we had been.

I picked up my things and helped him tuck himself back in his carriage, and then wiped the wet snowflakes off the tip of his fur. For a moment, I tightened my lip, and lifted my belongings up on my shoulders, careful to maintain my equilibrium, so that Coconut would not tumble back out again.

Then I stared in amazement as the snowflakes stopped falling and switched directions completely. It was just as my father had written. The blizzard was twirling upwards instead of down from the sky.

"Oh, we're in Aruna all right," I said gleefully. "Well, at least we made it, although I don't have a clue as to where we are."

"Are we lost?" Coconut questioned, twisting his neck to see in the distance.

"Not, yet. We should be able to find the Mecca of ice if we keep moving."

"How big is this place?"

"I don't really know, but it is larger than Kwata Calmoon. That's for sure," I said, staring down at the arctic blue water. I was wondering where the watercourse would lead.

Opening my mind, I quickly emerged the journal. Flipping through the pages, I finally settled on the best utility for the trip. Then, closing the booklet, I made visible from memory, a wooden canoe. This was no regular canoe, but one with motorized self-rowing paddles: just what we needed for the long journey ahead.

Steadying the craft, I stepped inside and sat down gently, directly, in the center seat. Immediately I removed the backpack, setting it down on the bottom of the boat. With a quick thrust of a row, the canoe paddles began a clockwork motion taking us speedily down the narrow canal.

It grew dark and the stars began to show in the night sky.

After the brisk snowfall stopped, I could see further up the river. Little by little, I began to make out a blurry image on the banks. I couldn't quite tell what it was, so I held out my hands and made the binoculars appear.

"What is it?" Coconut asked anxiously.

"Shh, I think its an animal," I said hastily, changing the focus.

As the craft drew near, I could make out a large water buffalo taking a sip near the edge of the river. "Water buffalo," I whispered excitedly.

"You sure?" Coconut said doubtfully. "You sure its not some kind of alien?"

"I ought to know a buffalo when I see one," I said.

The buffalo looked up from his drinking, icicles meshed in his chin, as he turned to run up the hill. "Come on, let's follow him. Maybe there are more life forms this way," I said, grabbing the backpack and jumping quickly from the watercraft.

I ran after the buffalo for a good two miles before we reached the top of the hill. Then I stood there open-mouthed, staring at the large flock of buffalo as they ran, skipped and frolicked in the snow. "This is good," I said. "*This is very good.*"

I remained standing for a while, wondering how long I could put up with the cold weather. Coconut was beginning to become a little restless, too, as the frost began to catch a hold of his limbs.

Suddenly, I gasped, happily. "Look, there among the

trees," I said, pointing.

A few feet ahead I saw a human form walking silently into a grove of pines. I followed the figure, shuffling through the deep snow, creeping past the buffalo, making my way into the forest. I could never seem to get any closer than when I first began the chase. This made no sense, for I was moving at a much faster speed than the being.

"HEH! *Wait!*" I yelled, unsure if I was doing the right thing. I had to squint to see as the snow began building up again. There was no response. I kept up the pace, never completely losing sight of the stranger, a female. This I could tell, because of the long dark hair, and Native American dress and moccasins she wore. Still, I could not yet glimpse her face.

I hesitated. Then, as I drew nearer, I began to get nervous.

Suddenly, she stopped, and turned to look at me. Her face seemed familiar. She was leading me somewhere.

Again she vanished and became visible again. She appeared a few feet ahead of me. She moved like a phantom, keeping a measurable distance. Her hair blew wildly and blended with the wind.

The blustery weather made the leaves fall in harmony with the crystals of snow, obscuring the path. Somehow, I managed to keep up, following her for several miles until she vanished completely at the edge of a valley.

My heart pounding, I came upon the clearing, then without thinking, ran towards the sparkles of light that formed the shape of a being. It was her, my great, great, grandmother Kanelia. I could feel her as her essence went through me. Mystic déjà vu, I thought keenly. She smiled at me warmly, and pointed in the distance.

"*Make ready your mind*," she whispered tenderly. "Behold, you are *already* there."

Slowly she began to fade away with the snowstorm, revealing a Mecca; the one I had been seeking.

MECCA OF ICE

Mystic Deja has to find her father, Octavius, before he passes through the next doorway, where he may never be found. Accomplishing this goal means traveling on a dangerous path, over a frozen lake to the Timoe Dali, and into the underground caverns where the shapeshifters live. Thankfully, she has a band of yabosaur allies that will go out of their way to make sure she arrives safely.

Now there are new aliens to battle, and more unusual weather, as well as new places to explore. Great Reign, the most powerful Emergist and conqueror of realms, is out to stop her from ruining his plans. Great Reign has a secret disguise, and an even more devious android creation; a new breed of silver assassins, hot on her trail.

Octavius is searching to enter his mind's eye, hoping to see his wife, Jenasee, one last time. But will this fantasy be his demise, or will Mystic Deja reach him in time?

About The Author

Originally from Grambling, Louisiana, Tina M. Randolph graduated from the Art Institute of Houston with an Associates Degree in Visual Communications. After graduation she worked as a computer graphic artist, editorial assistant, and later art director for several small magazines. She then went back to college and earned another Associates in Computer Information Systems.

For the past four years she has worked as a web designer and developer, specializing in multimedia and streaming video. She now spends most of her time reading, writing, and studying 3D animation and special effects. Randolph lives in Houston, Texas with her dog Gipsey.

www.ingramcontent.com/pod-product-compliance
Lightning Source LLC
LaVergne TN
LVHW021717060526
838200LV00050B/2721